Demonkeeper

By ROYCE BUCKINGHAM

G. P. Putnam's Sons

G. P. PUTNAM'S SONS
A division of Penguin Young Readers Group.
Published by The Penguin Group.
Penguin Group (USA) Inc., 375 Hudson Street, New York, NY 10014, U.S.A.
Penguin Group (Canada), 90 Eglinton Avenue East, Suite 700, Toronto,
Ontario, Canada M4P 2Y3 (a division of Pearson Penguin Canada Inc.).
Penguin Books Ltd, 80 Strand, London WC2R 0RL, England.
Penguin Ireland, 25 St. Stephen's Green, Dublin 2, Ireland
(a division of Penguin Books Ltd.).
Penguin Group (Australia), 250 Camberwell Road, Camberwell, Victoria 3124,
Australia (a division of Pearson Australia Group Pty Ltd).
Penguin Books India Pvt Ltd, 11 Community Centre, Panchsheel Park,
New Delhi - 110 017, India.
Penguin Group (NZ), Cnr Airborne and Rosedale Roads, Albany, Auckland 1310,
New Zealand (a division of Pearson New Zealand Ltd).
Penguin Books (South Africa) (Pty) Ltd, 24 Sturdee Avenue, Rosebank,
Johannesburg 2196, South Africa.
Penguin Books Ltd, Registered Offices: 80 Strand, London WC2R 0RL, England.

Design by Marikka Tamura. Text set in Minister Book.
Library of Congress Cataloging-in-Publication Data
Buckingham, Royce. Demonkeeper / Royce Buckingham. p. cm.
Summary: When Nat, the weirdest boy in Seattle, leaves for a date with the plainest girl
in town, chaos breaks out in the houseful of demons of which he is the sole guardian.
[1. Demonology—Fiction. 2. Supernatural—Fiction.] I. Title.
PZ7.B879857Dem 2007   [Fic]—dc22   2006026541   ISBN 978-0-399-24649-4
1 3 5 7 9 10 8 6 4 2
First Impression

*For my incredible, supportive parents,
a pair of which every child should have.*

For my incredible, supportive wife, Cara.

For Aspen and Aiden.

Thanks to Stephen King for scaring me silly.

*And thanks to all my friends
who read my stuff along the way . . .*

PROLOGUE

The Beast stretched out its thick limbs in the darkness. It flexed its claws like a great cat as it rose from the bone-scattered floor of its cave. Hunger gnawed at its belly. Of course it was always hungry, even after it gobbled up the bloody fish guts shoveled down its feeding chute each morning. It craved *live* food, but over time it had come to understand that there would be no fresh meat while it languished in this prison.

Even its simple brain remembered the old man that had trapped it down here so long ago. The old man had been clever, and powerful in a way the Beast did not understand. But there had been a change upstairs recently. The Beast no longer heard the old man's shuffling footsteps on the wood floors overhead. There was only one set of human feet tromping about now. Lighter, younger feet. A mere boy was minding its huge cell.

The Beast moved to the feeding chute. With a new Keeper there might be an opportunity to get out into the world of humans. It salivated as it began the long climb up the chute. Out in the world of humans there would be plenty of lost children to eat. . . .

CHAPTER 1

A Lonely Boy

I'm lonely, Nat thought. For almost a month now he'd been keeping the demons by himself. He crossed the large foyer of his old Craftsman-style Seattle home carrying two buckets of slop. Demon food. Fish entrails mostly, but they liked the heads too. They considered eyeballs a delicacy.

Nat stumbled over the huge, mustard-colored Indian rug. A few drops of the bloody mixture leapt from the bucket onto the floor and ran through a crack into the basement. Nat didn't notice. He was so deep in thought that he nearly tripped over a large, furry creature in the shadowy hall.

"Whoa!" He caught his balance. "Morning, Bel."

The massive English sheepdog, Belvedere, lifted one ear and peeked out at him through his mop of hair. "Sorry," Nat said, "in my own world this morning. Don't worry, I'll get your breakfast as soon as I feed the troublemakers."

Nat was glad he wasn't completely alone. At least he had Bel. Dhaliwahl had left him one friend that wasn't from the netherworld.

The hallway leading from the foyer was lined with antiques. Nat passed a scallop-backed wooden bench with carved heads at each of its peaks. The heads in the bench started up, greeting him with a ghostly chorus.

"Nathanieeel."

"Nathanieeeeel."

"Nathaaaaaaaaniel."

"Morning, morning, morning," Nat replied in turn as he walked by.

A lifeless plant on an ornate stand was next. Nat grabbed a watering can and dribbled a few drops on its brown leaves as he passed. It turned a vibrant green and began to overflow its pot behind him.

Nat didn't get three more steps before he heard a horrible groan of agony.

"Oo-aah . . ."

He tried to ignore it.

"Ooo-aaahh!" More insistent this time. He'd almost gotten past the masks.

The groan came from an iron one hanging on the wall.

The wooden mask directly across the hall from the iron mask scowled. "Why don't you shut up?" it grumbled. "It's the same groan every day, 'oo-oo-oooh, ah-ah-ahhh.' "

"Hey, I'm being tormented here," the iron mask snapped back. "Y'know what it feels like to rust?"

The wooden mask's bulging eyes rotated toward Nat. "Nat, you gotta move me. This guy's drivin' me crazy!"

"Oh no—I have seniority," argued the iron mask. "If anyone's moving, it's me."

Nat snatched the wooden mask from its nail on the wall. He couldn't separate them. Bickering audio possessions had to be kept in pairs, or they would hassle their Keeper rather than each other. Instead, he quickly switched the two, hanging each on the other's nail, then picked up his buckets and hurried on, leaving them frowning, puzzled, and staring straight at each other just as they had before.

Behind Nat, a lump rose in Bel's fur. A pair of yellow eyes peeked from the shaggy sea of hair, watching Nat's receding legs. Bel yawned and scratched once. His powerful hind paw ejected a fist-size creature. Its lumpy, misshapen body sprouted legs, and it scuttled after Nat, hiding in shadows. Nat paused to look around once, suspicious, but saw nothing. He shrugged and continued down the hall with his buckets.

Nat stepped into a bathroom with no proper sink

or toilet but only a long cast-iron trough. He began to empty one of his buckets of red slop into the trough.

Nat had a natural sense for demons. The hairs on the back of his neck usually stood on end when one was near and acting up. But the demon tracking him now could always surprise him. It peeked around the corner and began to morph into its true form. It stretched and contorted until it was a green, shin-high, schnauzer-snouted gargoyle with long, slender ears that stood straight up and paws that were as nimble and delicate as those of a raccoon. Oversized fangs jutted out from beneath its upper lip like twin daggers, and it sniffed after Nat with a twitching nose.

The thing eyed Nat's leg hungrily, then sprang, grabbing Nat's pants and pulling itself upward.

Nat yelped, trying to shake off the clinging monster. He whirled and looked down. It was Pernicious, the demonic incarnation of nasty surprises.

Nat took a deep breath and shook his head. "One more time, Pernicious, just one more, and I will exorcise your little butt back to the dimension that spawned you!"

Pernicious grinned, knowing that Nat would never do it. He leapt off Nat's leg with a high-pitched squeal. "Yee-hee-hee-heee!" He landed in the trough, buried his head in the fish parts, and began gorging.

Nat emptied the rest of the slop around him. "You're just lucky I'm new at this," Nat said. "An experienced Keeper would put you in your place."

Just then, thunderous footfalls sounded down the hall—the ominous thumping of an approaching monster. *Boom! Boom! Boom!*

The creature appeared at the corner. It was Nikolai, a thick little brute with rounded shoulders, stocky legs, and heavy eyebrows. He was shaped like a miniature Russian weight lifter, but his peaked ears and pointed muzzle lined with equally pointed teeth belied his demonic essence. Nik was only eight inches tall, but as he walked, his footsteps echoed about the room, ten times larger in sound than he was in size. Nik's nature was a bit of a mystery, but one thing was certain: he embodied the chaos of not knowing one's own strength. He'd once tried to help Nat fix a small drip in a pipe and crushed the entire thing in his grasp, sending water gushing through the house.

"G'morning, Nikolai," Nat said.

The mini-colossus leapt and grabbed the trough with a claw, hauling himself up with one thickly muscled arm.

"Dig in." Nat grimaced. The daily slop had a thick, warm smell, like bad milk, dead fish, and month-old tomato soup stirred together. "Don't wait for me."

Nik grunted and dipped his head into the bloody mixture.

Nat looked around. "Where's Flappy this morning?"

Even as he wondered, the little demon Flappy fluttered down the stairwell toward him on undersized reptilian wings. Flappy looked like a parrot-sized dragon and wobbled back and forth between the banister and paintings of distorted faces wailing in agony that hung on the opposite wall.

Flappy was a wind demon, the incarnation of swirling gusts—the aimless, spasmodic sort that sent children's kites into trees. At his size, he didn't seem dangerous, but Nat knew that wind demons could grow massive in the wild. They were known to down airplanes and violently send ships to watery graves. Fortunately, Flappy was too small and discombobulated to realize his own destructive potential.

Nat heard the frantic beating of wings outside the bathroom door just before Flappy flew through it in a zigzag flurry of scaly limbs. Nat ducked, Nik and Pernicious dove for cover, and Flappy somersaulted into the slop with a *splash*.

Nat peeked over the edge of the trough. Flappy sat up, dripping and bewildered, then plucked a salmon head and gulped it down pelican style. Seeing that Flappy was getting the choice bits, Pernicious and Nik dove back in and resumed their feast.

Nik, Pernicious, and Flappy were Nat's "minions"— those personal demons that had a special connection with their Keeper. They were supposed to assist him, but Nat wasn't so sure. They seemed to be more trouble than help.

Slurp, munch, gobble! The three little demons grew more frenzied with each bite. Flappy's wings beat at the slop and splattered red goo on the walls. Pernicious pilfered food from the others until Nik caught hold of him and dunked him in the muck.

Nat waved and gestured, trying to restore order without getting slimed. "Hey, stop that. Calm down . . ."

Snarfle, chomp, blurp!

"Listen to me," he pleaded.

A fish head flew out and struck Nat square in the chest. Nat watched it slide slowly down his shirt, leaving a slime trail. He slumped.

"You never behaved like this with Dhaliwahl," he said.

The three little heads snapped up, suddenly reverent and somber. Nat softened. "I'm sorry. I know. I miss him too."

All four stood and observed a moment of silence.

"But I'm in charge now, I guess," Nat continued, "so if you could please just try to take me seriously, that would be really helpful."

The three little demons bobbed their heads for a moment, appearing to understand. Then Nikolai burped ten times louder than his size. "Blaaaaat!"

Pernicious screeched with laughter. "Yee-hee-hee!" And the frenzy was on again.

Nat shook his head, defeated. He took the second pail and slunk out of the room to perform the next, and most unnerving, chore on his list.

Nat crossed the foyer to check the four heavy dead bolts on the basement door. The basement door was old but solid—forged from iron mined in the hills of southern Malaysia. He checked the bolts, then turned and waved his hand at the huge Indian rug. It undulated aside to reveal a hidden trapdoor in the floor that led to the feeding chute.

Nat found the trapdoor secure, its heavy iron bar in place, and he put his ear to it. He'd heard the Beast try to climb up the chute before. Today it seemed quiet. He took a deep breath, lifting his bucket into position. He slid the bar aside carefully, then he threw open the trapdoor and began dumping bloody sludge through a metal grate and down the three-sided chute as fast as he could.

While Nat poured the slop, Pernicious wandered into

the foyer behind him. The nearby fan was on. Pernicious watched its whirling blades and, being a mischievous little demon, couldn't resist sticking his finger in.

BRRRUD-DUD-DUD-DUD!

Nat spun around and poured bloody slop on his pants. "Pernicious!" He gave the little demon a severe frowning, and he was just beginning to wonder what sort of detergent would get fish blood out of tan cotton fabric when he felt the hairs on the back of his neck stand up.

An inhuman growl rose from below. *Wham!* Something slammed against the grate.

Nat fell backward, and the bucket flew, showering him with fish guts. As Nat wiped entrails from his eyes, the metal grate began to give way.

Wham! Wham! Wham!

Nat opened his eyes. He gasped. The grate was loose, hanging by a single screw. He tried to scramble away, slipping on blood and slime just as a monstrous claw burst through the grate and grabbed his leg. Its yellowed nails tore through his pants and into his calf. It hurt, badly.

The claw dragged him toward the half-open trapdoor. Nat grabbed in vain at the smooth wood floor. To his horror, he realized he was being pulled into the basement. He opened his mouth to scream, but his voice had abandoned him.

Nikolai arrived in the foyer and stared stupidly. Flat on his stomach, Nat could only wave one frantic hand. Nik trundled over and grabbed Nat's free leg to help. The little demon set his clawed feet in the wood floor and, using strength ten times his miniature size, he began to inch backward, pulling Nat into painful splits.

"Ahhhh!" Nat cried.

Pernicious darted up onto Nat's rump to survey the situation. Flappy flew in to lend a talon but only managed to slam into Pernicious.

"You're not helping!" Nat yelled as he clawed at the floor. The brutish hand from the basement was pulling him steadily toward the opening, and his foot was about to disappear into the feeding chute, no doubt to be quickly gobbled off. *That's it,* thought Nat, *I'm about to become the shortest-lived Demonkeeper in history.* He closed his eyes, resigned to his fate, just as—

Wham!

The huge paws of Bel fell upon the back of the trapdoor, slamming it down on the wrist of the claw. The beastly fingers released for an instant, and Nat scrambled away. Without a hold on Nat's leg, the huge arm slid back into the depths whence it came.

Nat quickly regained the wits that had been scared out of him. He dove forward to throw the bar across the trapdoor, then collapsed, panting. A receding rattle of metal and wet gargling of fish guts told him that the Beast was climbing back down the feeding chute into its prison. It was over.

Nat lay on his stomach for a time, wide-eyed, with sweat pouring off him. Finally, he turned to Bel. "That's just great, huh? My first month in charge of feeding, and *I* almost get eaten."

CHAPTER 2

A Lonely Girl

Sandra Nertz sat at the library reference desk holding a copy of *Practical Teen* magazine. Sandy's hair was pulled into a tight bun, her clothes were tidy and plain, and her reading glasses made her eyes bug out just a little.

But Sandy wasn't reading *Practical Teen*. She was sneaking a peek at *U Go Girl!*, the magazine "by Grrrlz 4 Grrrlz." *U.G.G.* was too cheesy for her—she was a sophomore now, after all, and a junior assistant librarian to boot. But when the seventh-grade girl had tossed it across the counter, it had fallen right into her lap and the cover had stared up at her accusingly. It said, *No Dates? Maybe It's U!* Sandy had resisted for nearly an hour. She almost couldn't bring herself to read it— she usually made fun of the girls who read such fluffy stuff. But almost every one of those girls, she noticed, came into the library with something she'd never had—a boyfriend.

Finally, Sandy checked over both shoulders, pulled up her copy of *Practical Teen,* and tucked *U Go Girl!* inside. When she was certain nobody was nearby, she flipped to the *No Dates?* survey.

The survey was written simply, with a lot of oversized exclamation points. Sandy studied the questions and carefully checked boxes. *Flat hair?* Check. *Less than ten bucks' worth of makeup in your bathroom?* Check. *Ears not pierced?* Check. *Disfiguring glasses?* Insulting, but check. *Your female doctor is the only person to ever see your cleavage?* Check.

The list went on. Sandy checked boxes, puzzling over such questions as, *Do you prefer a good book at home to a mediocre night out?* She pursed her lips. That one seemed downright unfair. But check. On it went. Check, check, check.

At the end of the survey, Sandy counted her checks, wincing at how many *yes* boxes she'd marked. Her score was fifty-two out of a possible sixty. She'd saved some points on question twenty-one, because she worked at a place "where people hang out." But she'd gained them right back when she was penalized for having a cat instead of a guy to hang out with after work. A top score was ten or less. For that score, the chart read *U R Un-*

forgettable. No dice. The eleven-to-twenty-point category declared *U R Memorable.* Nope. Twenty-one to thirty meant *U R Noticeable.* She came to the final category, scores of thirty to forty. It was titled, *And U Were . . . ?*

Sandy slumped in her chair. She was forgettable, pathetic even. *U Go Girl!* had proved it through standardized testing. The article didn't even have a category for over fifty—she was off the hopelessness charts.

Then she noticed that the article continued on the next page—it gave advice for girls who scored forty and up. It said, *The simple fix for forgotten chix is* adventurosity. Sandy wrinkled her nose. She was certain *adventurosity* was not a real word. She read on. *So why are U still sitting there? Adventurize! Take a chance! Ask out the next cute boy you see! U go girl!*

When Sandra Nertz looked up, there in the lobby, shaking water from himself like a dog, stood Nat.

Sandy cocked her head, looking him over as she absently organized the pencils in her cup from tallest to smallest. Nat pushed through the turnstile. It spun and hit him in the butt. *Perfect,* she thought, *not too intimidating, and kind of cute in a naive way.*

Thumpa-thumpa-thumpa!

Sandy's head jerked around as a kid skateboarded past the reference desk. Another boy followed sheepishly, carrying his board and a backpack with an anarchy symbol on it. The second boy was Richie, a street kid Sandy knew and liked. Sandy knew the first boy too. Gus. She did not like him.

"Hey! This is a board-free zone, you little miscreants!" Liz, the other assistant librarian, appeared at the end of the reference desk. Liz was a senior at Sandy's high school, the kind of girl who would have done well on the U.G.G. survey. Liz was definitely noticeable, possibly even memorable. She sashayed along the desk in tight pants, sticking out her noticeable chest. She sported a side-nostril nose ring and had a tattoo of barbed wire around her upper arm. She looked more like a young woman working at Hot-Mod Fashions in Westlake Center Mall than a teenage assistant librarian.

Liz walked up behind Sandy and grabbed the microphone for the library intercom. "Sandra Nertz, paging Sandra Nertz!"

Sandy jumped, spilling pencils.

Liz nodded toward the library entrance where Nat stood. "Weird patron at two o'clock."

"His name's Nathaniel," Sandy said, hiding *U Go Girl!* "He's been coming here for a couple of weeks. He seems nice."

"That guy?" Liz contorted her face. "He's genuinely creepy. Checks out books on the occult, witchcraft, do-it-yourself cremation . . ."

"Maybe he's just gothic."

Liz elbowed her. "Hey, if you think he's so nice, maybe you two can go out, get married, and move into a little mausoleum together with a black picket fence."

Sandy looked over at Nat. "I don't think he gets out much."

"Perfect," Liz said, "neither do you." Liz wandered off whistling a happy tune.

Sandy's face fell. She looked down at her safe, careful clothes.

When she looked up, Richie was standing at the reference desk with a guilty expression. "I, um, missed the free book giveaway," he said.

"Yes, and I missed you at the free book giveaway," Sandy replied. "It's okay—I saved a couple for you." She reached behind the desk and handed him *The Hobbit* and *The Phantom Tollbooth*.

Richie checked to make sure Gus wasn't watching and tucked the books in his pack.

Across the room, Gus was tearing magazine pages out to make paper airplanes. He looked up and waved Richie over. Richie nodded to Sandy and went to Gus.

Liz stood at the reference desk shaking her head. "You bought those books."

"There weren't any good free ones left," Sandy said.

"C'mon, Sandy, you can't rescue every stray that wanders in here."

Just then, Nat stumbled up to the reference desk.

"Hello." Sandy smiled. "What can I help you with today?"

Nat looked up as though just realizing where he was. "Huh? Oh! Yes." He rummaged his pockets with jittery hands and eventually produced a well-laundered piece of paper. "I'm looking for a book by this man. I don't know the title."

Sandy took the shred of paper. The writing was tough to make out, but she was accustomed to getting crumpled notes from kids.

Sandy turned to the computer. Her fingers flew. The citation popped up on her screen moments later, and she threw her hands in the air like an Olympic gymnast at the end of her routine. "Yes!" she cheered. Then she shrugged, sheepish. "I got it."

Nat leaned forward but didn't let himself get too close to her.

Sandy wrinkled her nose. "*Exercising Your Demons*. Is this a misspelled self-help book?"

"More of a training manual," Nat said.

Behind Nat, Liz silently mouthed the word "weirdo" to Sandy and wandered off.

"Wow, it's ancient," Sandy said, "and, uh-oh, it's only translated into Latin. Do you speak Latin?"

Nat shook his head.

"I know a little," Sandy said. "I could help you."

"Really? You'd help a 'weirdo'?"

Sandy wondered how Nat knew what Liz had mouthed to her. Perhaps there *was* something weird about him. Then Nat pointed to the citation on the computer, and Sandy saw that Liz would have been reflected in the screen. Mystery solved. "There's only one copy of this in the nation," she said. "I can have it for you in three weeks."

"Great! Thank you . . ."

"I'm Sandy. And there's the one-dollar interlibrary loan fee."

"Right. Of course," Nat said. He nodded and began dumping dimes, quarters, nickels, lint, and an *inspected by* tag out onto Sandy's pristine desk.

Sandy couldn't help herself—she stacked the coins by denomination, then hurried the lint and tag to the garbage.

Nat smiled as he watched her fuss.

Sandy realized he was watching and looked up. Their eyes met. *U go girl!* she thought. She took a deep breath. "You know, you've been coming here for a little while, and I never see you with anyone."

"I don't know a lot of people."

"You know me . . . now." She scribbled on his inter-library loan receipt. "You could call my cell."

"Your cell?"

"My phone."

Nat debated. He looked pained. "I'm not supposed to," he said finally.

"What? Like there's some rule against it?"

Nat took his receipt. "Yes," he said quickly, and he fled before she could say another word.

Sandy watched him go, sad. She didn't know how *U Go Girl!* would rate her effort to adventurize, but she imagined that, because the first boy she'd gotten the courage to proposition had run away, it wouldn't be good.

CHAPTER 3

The Coming of the Thin Man

The main crossing between Canada and Washington State was on Interstate 5, between Seattle and Vancouver, British Columbia. Twenty miles to the east there was a smaller checkpoint, much smaller. It was so small, in fact, that Customs Agent Mozelewski sometimes didn't see a car for fifteen minutes at a time. And he couldn't remember the last time someone had come through his checkpoint on foot.

That morning a heavy fog had rolled in, quickly enveloping the customs booth like a huge white catcher's mitt. If Mozelewski had not left the booth to turn on the supplemental warning lights, he would have never even seen the Thin Man.

The slender figure that emerged from the fog walked directly down the center of the road. The mist swept after the shadowy man as though in sinister league with him. He wore a long coat, but it didn't hide the fact that he was horribly gaunt. At first, Mozelewski thought his eyes must be playing tricks. Besides being impossibly thin, the man's bony hand appeared, for a moment, to be on fire. Then Mozelewski blinked, and he no longer saw any flames.

Mozelewski held up his hand, signaling for the man to stop. For a moment, it seemed the Thin Man might completely ignore the large agent, but Mozelewski stepped directly in his path. Mozelewski waved the persistent fog away to get a better look at him. The man's hair was jet black but wispy, as though it should have long since turned gray. His inky, unblinking eyes were entirely black and set deep in cavernous sockets. They seemed to suck the light in and not let it out. But he didn't appear blind. To the contrary, Mozelewski felt like the man was looking right through him. And though expressionless, the man also seemed like the *how-dare-you-stop-me* type.

"Destination?" Mozelewski asked in a cheery tone.

The man thought it over, not, it seemed, because he didn't know the answer, but because he wasn't sure he needed to bother with such an inconvenience as answering questions. Mozelewski had seen his kind before.

Finally, the man spoke, sort of. The sound that came out of his throat was more like an evil hiss than a voice, almost that of a human snake.

"Ssseattle," hissed the man.

"And where do you call home, sir?" Mozelewski smiled. Because of his size, Mozelewski didn't need to be gruff.

"Wherever I am," the man whispered.

"Your citizenship, smart guy," Mozelewski said, just a touch less polite.

"I've dwelled in Canada for decadesss," the Thin Man said, "biding my time, waiting for . . ."

Mozelewski didn't have time for his life story. They were standing in the middle of a foggy road, and a car could arrive any minute. The strange guy was Canadian. Good enough. "Okay, fine. And the purpose of your visit to the United States today?"

"To claim an ancient home that is rightfully mine. Itsss former owner hasss graciousssly passsed on."

"Real estate deal, eh? Anything to declare?"

It was a standard question, but the man seemed perplexed. "Anything to declare?" Mozelewski repeated more slowly.

Finally, the man raised his arms. "I am the massster of chaosss!"

"And I'm the prince of Poland." Mozelewski frowned. "Any alcohol?"

The Thin Man's eyes narrowed. He shook his head.

"Tobacco?" Mozelewski asked. "Cash over five thousand dollars?"

As the man glared, smoke began to roll from his nostrils.

"Native fruit . . . ?"

• • •

Mozelewski fled into the customs booth and slammed the door, terrified. A wall of pulsating, amoebic green goo slammed against the door behind him, gumming it closed. Moments later, living flames licked up around the booth.

The Thin Man strode through the checkpoint as the booth burned. He grinned and motioned over his shoulder.

The ground split open under the booth. The building lurched into the crack. Mozelewski's face pressed against the glass, and he uttered a silent scream. The fissure widened, the small building fell in, then the crack eased shut, trapping the large agent inside.

The Thin Man waved off the fog. He did not want a car to strike him. If a car hit him, there would be attention from the authorities and possibly even injuries to his human body. Such things would be most inconvenient just now. The fickle fog had failed in its purpose to conceal him through the border anyway.

As the Thin Man walked, the fissure in the ground chased after him. It was Wedge, the insidious demonic crack whose nasty habit was to travel through inanimate objects, find their faults, and wrench them apart. Wedge tore through the ground between the Thin Man's feet and preceded him like a leash with no dog, heralding his ominous coming.

The flame demon Charr zipped through the brush after its master and leapt onto the back of his coat. Charr was a great destroyer, a devourer. It burned up over the coat and nestled in the Thin Man's palm like a living fireball.

The green, sticky demon of foul fluids was Goop, a Quagmirian Congealment of the Second Order. Goop delighted in lurking in dim, dank places—garbage bins, public restrooms, nasal cavities—whence he could ooze out over the hand or foot of anyone unlucky enough to get close. Goop lacked the sheer destructive power of Charr and Wedge but was easily the most disgusting of the group.

Goop hurried to catch up with the others. It coagulated into a viscous little gelatin blob, then undulated up the Thin Man's leg, under his coat, over his neck, and around his ear and poured itself up into his left nostril.

These were his three minions. They rode him or followed him wherever he went. He kept them close and drew strength from their chaotic energy. In turn, he directed their destructive powers toward a common purpose. Presently, that purpose was to find an old house full of similar creatures in the drizzliest city in the United States. The Thin Man set his jaw with grim determination and marched past a sign that read SEATTLE—100 MILES.

CHAPTER 4

Duty and Responsibility

It was not exactly raining, but the air was damp. Seattle was like that, almost cheery but with something dark lurking just below the surface.

Nat walked through his Queen Anne Hill neighborhood. He had a nasty cut in his leg where the Beast had grabbed him. The demons never seemed to get to Dhaliwahl, but keeping them was hard for Nat. Why couldn't he have a normal teenage job, he thought, like flipping burgers? Sure, rancid french fry grease was smelly, but so were demons, and at least the customers he served wouldn't try to eat him.

He turned onto his own street. He'd walked this route every day with Dhaliwahl not so long ago. Dhaliwahl would shuffle along with his staff, which had a carved Indian cobra head on top.

If Dhaliwahl were still around, he would have something to say about today's trip to the library. Certainly something about girls. His mentor had expressed strong feelings on *that* topic.

"No, young Nathaniel," Nat recalled Dhaliwahl's thick East Indian accent, "no Keeper has ever married that I know. Marriage is attempting stability. To be a Keeper is wrestling always with chaos. They do not mix. If you wish to be Demonkeeper, keep your mind on your demons, yes?"

"So no girls at all?"

"Forget them. They are not demons," the old man mumbled dismissively. "Only the succubus appears in the female form. A nasty parasite that seduces men in their beds, then bites them." Dhaliwahl snarled for emphasis. "Your duties are more important than all the fuss that is made over girls," he continued. "They seem like big fun. Oh, don't I know it. But demons can drive you to madness, and nothing will help drive you mad more quickly than a female."

So that was the rule. No girls. At least that was Dhaliwahl's rule.

Nat walked up the street where his massive 1901 home loomed over the otherwise tidy neighborhood. Its paint was peeling, and its lawn was overgrown. Next door, his neighbor, Mr. Neebor, knelt in his tidy, well-ordered garden. *Mr. Neebor does not like chaos,* thought Nat.

Nat didn't particularly enjoy running into Mr. Neebor. The man was nosy, he frowned a lot, and he was always going on about "property values." But Nat was in luck—Neebor was huddled close to his prize hydrangea and using tweezers to trim it. Nat tiptoed to his own gate, eased it open, and tried to slip inside.

"Hullo." The creaky old voice rose behind him like a rusty gear beginning to turn. He was caught.

"Uh, hi, Mr. Neighbor," he said without turning around.

"*Nee*-bor," complained Neebor. "*Nee-bor.* Say, where's that old blind fella? Ain't seen him for a week."

Nat slumped. "A month."

"You don't say. Been that long? Where'd he go?"

Nat turned to face Neebor. "Mr. Dhaliwahl is . . . well, he's gone." Nat swallowed a lump in his throat and continued. "Left me to fend for myself, I'm afraid."

"Oh. Shame. Shame and a pity." Neebor bowed his head for a moment, then peeked up at Nat hopefully. "Some aunt or uncle gonna come take you away then, I expect?"

Nat shook his head and pointed at his nightmare yard. "Oh no. I need to stay and keep up the house."

"By yourself? No grown-ups?"

"Oh my gosh!" exclaimed Nat, looking down at his

bare wrist as if he were wearing a watch. "I've got to get going."

Nat waved Neebor a quick farewell and hurried off, leaving his cranky old neighbor crinkle-browed over both what he had said and what he hadn't.

• • •

Nat stepped onto his porch, which shook happily, anticipating his return home like a faithful dog.

"Whoa, boy," Nat said, "you need to settle down before I climb you." Fortunately, the frisky porch was attached to the house. Nat couldn't imagine how he would ever corral the huge thing if it took off running down the street.

The steps calmed, and when Nat judged that he could walk up them without being thrown off by an enthusiastic quiver, he hustled to the door. Nat slid the giant exterior dead bolts loose, and the door swung open on its own, revealing the pitch-black entryway. Hundreds of yellow eyes stared out at him from the darkness, waiting for him to enter. The same sight had frightened him terribly the first time Dhaliwahl had brought him to the house. *How did I ever get up the courage to walk into this?* he wondered. But the answer had been simple back then. He had no place else to go.

• • •

Nat was only a boy when his parents' boat had been lost in a freak storm in the San Juan Islands. He was found bobbing in Puget Sound in the life jacket his mother had always insisted he wear. There was no next of kin. He was alone and adrift in the world.

The Agency for the Placement of Lost Children shipped him from place to place, but he never stayed anywhere long enough to make friends. He saw things wherever he went—the demons. If he spoke of them to his foster parents, they would usually make a hurried call, and the agency would move him again. He soon learned to keep his demons to himself.

Then one day the agency lost him. Suddenly, his name was no longer in their system. Oddly, that was the day Raja Dhaliwahl had shown up.

Dhaliwahl was sitting in the placement office when Nat's most recent host family returned him to the agency. When Nat walked in, the old man clapped and praised his own gods in Bengali. He walked Nat to the counter. That was when the agency could not find him in their computer. The woman at the front desk apologized, Dhaliwahl immediately showed her some strange documents, and she seemed perfectly happy to send Nat off, seeing as he was not in their computer anymore.

"I know that I cannot be your parents, young

Nathaniel," Dhaliwahl said when they arrived at the house. "I also know this place is strange to you, and until you grow confident that you belong here, you will be always the lost child you are today. But I can give you shelter and a purpose. These things may be of use to a boy such as you, yes?"

Nat nodded, stunned that an adult could be so direct and perceptive.

"This is very serious, for once a Keeper brings an apprentice into this world, there is much responsibility," Dhaliwahl said.

Nat looked at his feet. "I don't know if I'm up to it."

"I am meaning much responsibility," Dhaliwahl clarified, "for the Keeper."

•   •   •

Nat entered the darkness, and the door swung closed behind him. The lights came up, the eyes vanished, and Nat stood in the foyer as though he were a typical boy in a typical old house, except that the chair across the foyer fidgeted anxiously. Nat passed a wall clock the size of a beach ball. The hands read 11:30.

"Oh no!" He was late for mid-morning rounds. The demons would be restless. Then he frowned. "Wait a minute." He pointed at the clock, suspicious. The hands backed up exactly one minute. "All the way back." The clock moved back, reluctantly, to 10:30.

Nat nodded and turned just as Bel greeted him with a slobbery muzzle in the crotch.

"Hey!"

Nat shrugged out of his coat and opened the closet. "Know what, big boy?" Bel shook his head, flinging saliva left and right. "Something happened to me today."

A talon reached from the closet for Nat's neck. Nat dodged and hung his coat on the talon.

"I talked to a girl."

Bel frowned.

"I know, I know," Nat said, "I shouldn't have, but I did."

Nat turned and spoke gently to the fidgety chair. "Relax, fella," he told the chair. "You're free to roam. You don't have to hide here."

The chair lashed out like a spooked wildebeest, smacking Nat in the head with one leg and knocking him to the floor. It kicked up its heels several times and romped off down the hall. Nat rubbed his head.

"You know, Bel," he said, looking up, "Dhaliwahl never actually said I *couldn't* speak to girls. I mean, why should my duties keep me from having someone to talk to . . ." The shaggy dog sneezed, covering Nat's face with dog snot and drool, then Bel wandered off, leaving him alone and dripping. Nat sighed. ". . . that doesn't have paws or claws?"

Demonkeeper

CHAPTER 5

Wussy?

Richie and Gus held their skateboards and stood on the neatly trimmed grass behind Mr. Neebor's garage, peeking around at Nat's house. Richie was twelve, going on fifteen. Gus was fourteen, going on seven. Gus had a tall, green Mohawk hairdo and the word *screw* shaved into the buzz cut over one ear. When he turned, the other side of his head said *you*. He wore baggy clothes and a bull-style skull-'n'-crossbones nose ring through the flesh between his nostrils. Richie was a mild imitation—stringy hair, a beaten Seattle Mariners hat turned backward, baggy pants, and a black concert T-shirt for the band SLuG BaiT.

Gus smoked a cigarette. "See, dude," he said, "there's the weird kid's house. I saw him go in there."

Richie nodded.

"Want a puff?" Gus said.

"Those things'll kill ya," Richie said.

Gus laughed. His laugh was a thin, high-pitched squeal that sounded like someone slowly letting the air out of a balloon. "I gotta die someday, right?" Gus pointed at Nat's house. "The way I see it," Gus said, "the kid's parents have got to have some cool stuff in there. I mean, look at the place. It's straight out of a horror flick."

"And that's good?" asked Richie.

"Unless you're a wussy . . ."

Whenever Gus used the word *wussy,* a challenge was almost certainly coming. The last challenge Gus had issued had involved a skateboard ramp, a paper bag, dog turds, and a lit match; it hadn't turned out so good. Richie knew that he needed to stop hanging out with Gus before something really bad, not just disgusting, happened.

"I'm not a wussy," he said.

Gus grinned. "Then you'll come back here with me tonight and prove it, eh?"

A floorboard squeaked. The boys whipped around, surprised. Mr. Neebor stood on his porch holding his deluxe, variable pressure garden hose coiled over one arm. He aimed the nozzle at them.

"All right, you punks," he growled, giving them his best Clint Eastwood imitation, "get off the lawn."

"Oh yeah?" Gus said. "What are you going to . . . ?"

The first jet of water knocked the cigarette cleanly from Gus's mouth. The second blasted the lighter from his hand. Neebor cocked the hose to his ear, then leveled it again, this time at Gus's nose.

"Off . . . the lawn," Neebor repeated.

Gus and Richie turned and ran.

CHAPTER 6

Give Me a Break

Nat's kitchen represented wildly different eras. A wood-burning stove sat beside a microwave.

Nat walked in to rustle up some lunch. Nikolai handed him a piece of wood twice the little demon's size, and Nat dumped it into a hole in the lit stove. Flames licked up. Nik shrank in terror, then leapt across the room, bounced off a chair, and landed a safe distance away on the table.

"Sorry, Nik, should've warned you," Nat said. "But you don't have to be so scared of fire." Nik brooded atop the kitchen table. Nat tossed a frozen burrito in the microwave. As Nat held the door open and talked to Nik, Pernicious sent two long eyestalks around from behind the microwave to peek in through the door. He eyed the burrito, then crept forward.

Nat swung the microwave door closed without looking and flipped it on, unaware that Pernicious had slipped inside. "You know," he said to Nik, "most folks think demons like it hot."

The light came on as the microwave hummed to life. Inside, Pernicious stood atop the burrito with a hunk of frozen beans and cheese in his mouth. The little demon's eyes went wide with alarm. Pernicious began to turn red and melt, his features running like candle wax.

Nat retrieved a fork and a jar of salsa, whistling over the hum of the microwave and the faint squeals from inside. *Ding!* The timer went off. Nat opened the microwave and frowned. His burrito was already smothered in red sauce, and it had a bite out of it. Nat looked closer. There was a faint shape to the red goo, a vague, drippy face.

"Oh, man! What next?" Nat shook his head and retrieved a plastic bowl. "I swear I don't know how Dhaliwahl did it." He poured Pernicious's jellied remains into the bowl and put the bowl in the fridge. Pernicious's eyes were visible in the jelly, still alert and full of mischief but unable to do anything except float. He wouldn't be going anywhere anytime soon.

Nat plopped down at the table. For a moment it was quiet, and Nat almost relaxed. Then Nik lifted a huge cupboard with one hand to get at a scrap of food underneath. The glasses on the cupboard slid. Nat looked up just in time to see the first glass tumble toward the floor.

Crash! Other glasses followed. *Crash, crash . . . crash!*

Nikolai gave Nat a guilty look. *Wham!* He dropped the cupboard and scuttled out of the kitchen. A final glass still teetered. Nat didn't even bother lunging for it. . . . *Crash!*

I need a break, Nat thought. The only normal moment he'd had all day was when Sandy had asked him to call her, and he'd totally blown that opportunity. *If only I hadn't been such a coward and had taken her number,* he thought, absently crinkling in his pocket the interlibrary loan receipt that she'd given him.

CHAPTER 7

Asking Directions

The Thin Man stood at a fork in the road in north Seattle. He did not remember the crossroad. It had been many years since he'd left the Emerald City. Things had changed. The city had gotten bigger. *Good,* he thought. A master of chaos could do his best work shrouded in the anonymity of city crowds. But first he had to find his way back to the house.

He waved at a passing car. The car whizzed by without slowing. Another came. This time the Thin Man thrust an arm out, palm first. The car slowed to get a look at him. But when Charr peeked from his pocket and Goop oozed up to his shoulder for a better view, the car accelerated and raced past. Their heads turned with their master's to watch it go.

The Thin Man didn't really want to talk to humans,

but he needed to. When the next set of headlights came into view, he pointed at the road. Wedge leapt forward, tearing a great rent in the street. The asphalt parted, leaving a foot-wide trench of crumbled rock and tar.

The car hit the rupture and instantly blew its front tires. The driver turned the wheel and the car fishtailed, blowing the rear tires too, then sliding into the phone pole at the fork in the road.

Crash!

The Thin Man approached, strolling to the wreck as though out to collect his morning paper. *Humans are too easy,* he thought.

The vehicle was a crumpled ruin. The Thin Man stepped to the shattered driver's window and tapped the injured man on the shoulder. The driver's bruised and battered head lolled toward him. The Thin Man pointed to the Y in the road.

"Excussse me," he hissed, "which way is quickessst to Queen Anne Hill?"

CHAPTER 8

Nat Takes a Chance

Nat finished the afternoon chores and went to the study to try to find some peace. He drifted to the hearth and adjusted a simple clay urn on the mantel. Its inscription read *RAJA DHALIWAHL*. Nineteen more urns lined the mantel beyond Dhaliwahl's. They were golden, beaten copper, clay—each one a different shape. All bore names—Andre LeFevre, Yatabe the Wanderer, George McFeen, Vincent Lazano, Michael Jones Francis and many more. *DHALIWAHL* was the most recent. They were all represented on the shelf, each a link in the unbroken chain of Demonkeepers.

Demons had been around since before the dawn of mankind, lurking on the fringes of human senses. Humans with especially acute senses could see them, hear them, feel them, smell them, and probably taste them too (though Nat didn't know of any Keepers who had tried that). A select few of those special humans were recruited as apprentices to become Keepers. No one forced those with sight to become Keepers. It was simply a calling, and a calling could go unanswered—many seers went undiscovered, untrained, and never understood the manifestations of chaos they saw. Some went insane and gouged out their own eyes or lopped off an ear to cut their bridge to the madness.

Normal humans busily chased order and security, subconsciously ignoring chaos and the demonic goings-on around them. The average person might feel the presence of a low-level demon as a cold shiver, glimpse it in the shadows, or hear it as a vague noise in the attic. But high-level demons were more adept at concealing themselves and were more dangerous. Some killed.

Nat was fond of Keeper history. He recalled one of the stories of Yatabe the Wanderer that Dhaliwahl had told him. Yatabe had been a bold Keeper famous for his crazy schemes. Yatabe was the first to theorize that if you could force an audio demon, an apparition, and a possessory demon into the same object, you would have only one demon to keep instead of three. Of course, he failed to take into account that the single hybrid demon that resulted would be more than three times the trouble, because it could change appearance, make sounds, and move all at once. By the time his new strain of demon had led him on a destructive chase through an Asian village that prompted the residents to confront Yatabe with angry spears, he was sorry he had dabbled.

As Nat surveyed the urns, his eyes drifted to the huge book on a nearby pedestal. The book's yellowed pages were ancient, and the cracked leather cover read *DK*. The *DK Journal* was the official method of passing knowledge on to each apprentice. It had been around since the Age of Jamala. Prior to the *Journal,* the tradition had been passed down by word of mouth. The first thing that Jamala had written was an account of how he'd forgotten an important incantation and had nearly been flattened by a possessory demon of the Third Order that had taken over a horse cart. After that, important demonkeeping techniques were documented by the Keeper who perfected them. Unsuccessful attempts were noted too, if the Keeper was still around to write about them. For instance, it does no good to taunt an apparition with insulting remarks, because apparitions dwell on the visual plane of existence only and can't hear a thing.

Unfortunately, the journal was written in the language of each Keeper. Some were dead languages: Latin, Aramaic, Sanskrit. To learn the craft completely, one had to learn the writings of dozens of foreign and ancient peoples. So far, Nat only knew a couple. He knew English, of course, and his Bengali was okay. The others, not so good.

Nat slumped by the window. He pulled out the interlibrary loan receipt he'd shoved in his pocket on the way out of the library and took aim for the garbage can. But just before he threw it away, he saw that Sandy had scribbled something on it. It read 737-5467. Nat blinked. It was her phone number!

Nat reached for the old phone nearby, but the hairs on the back of his neck stood up, just as they did when demons were near, and he hesitated. He was supposed to avoid girls, and Nat had to admit that being around Sandra Nertz scared him a little. But Dhaliwahl had also told him that he must always face his fear. Given two conflicting rules, which should he follow? Should he avoid the girl or face his fear? He took a deep breath and dialed.

The call was answered. "Hello, this is Sandy."

The blood drained from Nat's face. Fear. He wondered if she could smell it like demons could. "Hello," he began, "is this Sandy?" Nat winced. She'd already given her name. "Stupid," he whispered at himself, "stupid, stupid, stupid."

"Nathaniel, is that you?"

"Um, yeah," he said.

"Wow," said Sandy, "I really didn't think you would call."

"Well, I, uh . . . I found your number and, um, and . . ."

". . . and maybe you'd like to ask me to go do something?" Sandy suggested.

There was a sudden mad clinking from the urns that sounded vaguely like giggling. Nat glared at them, covered the phone, and whispered fiercely, "Shut up, or I'll turn you into flowerpots!"

"Excuse me?" Sandy said.

Nat snapped his attention back to the phone. "I said, uh, 'show up.' Just 'show up and bring a flowerpot.'"

"Aw, that's sweet. And I just happen to be free tonight."

"Tonight?"

"I'll be by in a few minutes. Don't worry, I know where you live. It's on your library account."

"Oh," Nat said, shell-shocked.

"Bye-bye," Sandy said.

Nat hung up. Dripping with sweat, he unlocked the aging window nearby, forced it up for some fresh air and wiped his brow. Then he glanced across the room. Nik was squatting nearby, snorting demonically and digging in his ear with a gnarled claw.

"Oh no," Nat cried, "she can't come here!" He grabbed the *DK Journal* and rushed out, so flustered that he left the study window wide open.

CHAPTER 9

Preparing for a Guest

A ttention, everyone . . . attention!" Nat barked.

Suddenly, the house came alive with creaks, groans, whispers, and murmurs that seemed to originate from behind him, above him, and just around the corner at the same time. "For those of you that don't already know, a girl will be here soon." More twitters and rustling. "If you could just lay low for a little bit, that would be great."

A piece of decorative trim along the wall poked its legs out and scuttled away like a walking stick. It headed upstairs to spread the gossip.

"Could you stay hidden for just a few minutes? Please?"

Something flew out of the study—a large hardback book, flapping its cover like a pair of wings. Nat threw himself to the ground. The hardback swooped low through the foyer, just missing him.

Suddenly, the rug curled around Nat, trying to roll him up like a pig in a blanket. "Stop it!" he said.

He leapt clear just as an entire flock of paperbacks fluttered through the foyer, followed by a freestanding bookcase. It jumped and snapped its shelves at the fleeing books, trying to recapture them.

The carved heads started in. "NATHAAAANIEL," "NATHAAAAAAANIEL." Nat grabbed a roll of tape and slapped a piece over each mouth. "NATHA—"

He rushed to his bedroom. Even in his hurry, he paused at an old framed photo of himself as a grinning twelve-year-old between his mother and father. He whispered to his parents, "You'd like her."

Nik and Flappy sat atop his dresser. Nat picked up a small, ornate puzzle box and twisted the lid. The box was the size of a Rubik's Cube and functionally a cross between a genie bottle and a pet carrier. He motioned the demons inside. They stepped close, and the box sucked them in like a vacuum cleaner. Nat twisted the lid shut, grabbed his jacket, and took a deep breath.

"Okay, I've got my coat and my minions are in the box, but I know I'm forgetting something." *Something about a window,* he thought. He looked out the window

Demonkeeper

at the quiet street, the setting sun over the bay, and Mr. Neebor's pristine flower garden. . . .

• • •

Moments later, Nat was crawling on his hands and knees through Neebor's rosebushes and hydrangea. He didn't know what sort of flowers he should get for a date with a girl, but he thought he should find something colorful and, hopefully, something Neebor wouldn't miss. He chose some yellow flowers. He chose some red ones. He thought he should stop, but a few white ones seemed to go well with the yellow and red. A light came on in Neebor's house. Nat hit the dirt and froze. Then he heard something even more distressing. A car approaching. There was rarely traffic on his street. The car would be Sandy.

CHAPTER 10

Lurking, Waiting, Salivating

The Beast loped up the basement stairs and crouched by the iron door. It sharpened its curved claws on the door's metal surface with long, slow strokes.

The human boy beyond the door had left the house. It was times like these that the Beast tested the strength of the metal door. It worked daily on the trapdoor too, scratching, pushing, waiting.

The Beast salivated, recalling that it had almost gotten a taste earlier, a reward for hanging silently from the feeding chute all morning. But just as it was about to sink its teeth into the boy's warm, young flesh, something had pounded it on the back of the head. It rubbed its sloping skull and growled. It would look for another chance. The boy was careless, like most boys. He would make another mistake.

CHAPTER 11
Sandy Arrives

Sandy drove up to Nat's house in her parents' rusty old Volvo. She pulled forward and back several times, grinding gears together, and shuddered to a stop. It was parked. Badly.

Sandy stepped out, smoothed her ankle-length skirt, and adjusted her pink sweater. She'd tried to pick an outfit that was fun but still felt like she had missed the turn for church and ended up here. In her hands was a flowerpot.

Sandy squared up to the massive old house that rose against the San Juan Islands sunset. "Wow," she said. The house didn't match Nat exactly. Nat was only quirky, and the house was genuinely spooky. But this was her real first date. *Spooky or not,* she thought, *here I come,* and she pushed through the wrought-iron gate.

The walk was cracked and worn. Sandy never wore heels at school—they'd sat untouched in her closet for over a year. She stumbled as she picked her way up the path in the waning twilight, hopping from stone to stone on shoes that felt like tiny stilts, certain that Nat would eventually wonder where she was and walk outside to find her sprawled across his yard with two broken ankles.

She made it to the front steps without falling. But when she stepped up onto the porch, she felt it shift beneath her. She took another tentative step. It felt solid now. She looked up and discovered something else odd. The door had large bolts . . . on the outside.

Sandy turned and looked back at her car. She had a sudden urge to flee. What did she really know about this boy anyway? The practical thing to do would be to leave now and call to cancel from a safe distance. But she was adventurizing. She stepped to the door.

CHAPTER 12

A Girl in the House

Nat hurried to the long mirror in the entryway. He frowned. The mirror reflected Nat's clothes, but it showed his head as a white skull, and his hands were skeletal.

Nat didn't give the mirror the satisfaction of complaining. He simply adjusted his trousers with his bony fingers and smoothed his shirt. He took a deep breath and stepped to the front door.

Sandy was reaching to knock when Nat popped open the door.

"Oh!" she yelped, surprised. "Here you are."

"Hi," said Nat. He thrust a bunch of flowers through the crack. Sandy held out her pot. Nat slid the bouquet into it but didn't move from behind the door.

"Thank you," said Sandy. "They're gorgeous. Where did you get them?"

Nat rubbed his hands. Sandy watched fresh dirt cascade over her pristine shoes. "Nearby," he said.

They stood in awkward silence for a moment, each of them unsure exactly how they'd wound up standing at the threshold together.

"Can I come in?" Sandy suggested finally.

"No!" Nat said a little too firmly. "You really shouldn't. The place is a mess. You know, old house, lots of junk. I'll just grab some money." Nat disappeared and slammed the door in her face.

Sandy fidgeted, bewildered. She looked back at her car again, still debating. It was either this spooky house or home alone. *U go girl,* she thought. She took a deep breath, tucked her flowerpot under her arm, and reached for the doorknob.

Nat trotted into the dining room. A claw-foot banquet table ran its entire length. The table had been captured in an abandoned castle in Scotland long ago by Michael Jones Francis, the great English Keeper. In the *Journal,* Francis described finding three very dead treasure hunters around the huge table, all cut to pieces as if mauled by a lion.

Nat scooted around the room, back against the wall, careful not to disturb the massive thing. He tiptoed to a small chest. The chest was filled with diamonds, gold

Demonkeeper

coins, and assorted other treasures collected by Keepers over the centuries. As he grabbed a modern twenty-dollar bill, he heard the front door creak open.

"Oh no . . ."

He started back, but in his haste, he stumbled over a leg of the guardian table. To his horror, it moved. He dodged as one of the claws swiped at his leg, catching and ripping his pants. He dove out through the door and scrambled into the foyer on all fours, almost running headfirst into Sandy's kneecaps. He gasped. "Oh! My gosh. You're inside."

Sandy saw his torn pant leg. "Are you okay?"

"Yeah. Just snagged my pants on the table."

Sandy reached to help him up. He felt her hand in his and marveled at how slender it was. They stood staring at each other. Nat tried to speak. He couldn't.

Sandy looked around the foyer. "The things in here are incredible," she said. "Do your parents collect antiques?"

Nat looked away. "No. I, uh, recently inherited it all."

"*You* own this?"

"More like it owns me. You didn't touch anything, did you?" he asked.

"No," she said.

"And nothing touched you?"

Sandy shook her head, puzzled.

Nat caught her and ushered her back toward the front door. "We should get going."

In the shadows overhead, a paperback fluttered in a circle, honing in on them, positioning itself to dive. Sandy turned, looking for the source of the noise.

"Bats," Nat said.

Heavy footsteps echoed down the hall, approaching. *Thump-thump-thump!*

"Furnace," Nat snapped. "Shall we go?"

"Okay." Sandy shrugged.

In the kitchen, Pernicious slipped out of the plastic bowl, now congealed like a Jell-O mold gargoyle. He pushed open the fridge and scurried out into the foyer.

Nat was so busy trying to keep Sandy from spotting a dozen pieces of wall trim that had crawled loose that he didn't notice Pernicious.

Sandy tried to smile as Nat hustled her along. "Maybe next time you can show me the whole place?" she said.

Sandy stumbled out of the house and down the steps, Nat having given her a little extra shove at the threshold.

• • •

As Nat exited, Pernicious slipped out behind him, unseen, and darted for Sandy's car.

Regaining her footing, Sandy turned and stared

at Nat, bewildered. He fastened the locks both inside and out. Behind him, a huge commotion echoed inside the house.

Craaash!

Nat forced a smile as though he'd heard nothing. "So where do normal kids go?"

"You mean where do kids normally go?" Sandy said.

"Yeah, that's what I meant."

Sandy thought for a moment. "The mall?"

CHAPTER 13

Coming Home

*T*he Thin Man reached the bottom of Queen Anne Hill and looked up but didn't smile. This homecoming, of a sort, was bittersweet—mostly bitter.

He had not yet decided what to do when he reached the house. Dhaliwahl was no longer in his way. This much he knew. But chaos was a treacherous business. He wasn't sure what he would find when he got there. He might simply walk in and take over. Then again, there might be resistance. There would certainly be a new Keeper, an apprentice, to deal with. But he was prepared to do battle to take back what was rightfully his.

The Thin Man was confident in his abilities. His years away had been well spent. During that time, he had scoured British Columbia for demons, training himself to find them, control them, and even destroy them.

Killing was a skill no other Keeper had ever practiced. It was not allowed. But with no preaching mentor to stop him, he had learned to embrace chaos, become a part of it, and use its destructive force to his advantage. Now he was powerful in a way that no traditional Keeper could ever be.

He also had three minions, as many as the great Keepers. Most Keepers had one, a select few had two, but only those with exceptional ability, renowned Keepers such as Michael Jones Francis and Yatabe the Wanderer, had ever corralled three. It was written in the *Keeper's Journal* that multiple demons kept too close could drive a Keeper mad. *Bah,* he thought. He fed off their chaos. Channeling the chaotic power of three minions through himself gave him the strength to walk hundreds of miles without breaking a sweat. *And only a couple more miles to go,* he thought.

The Thin Man started up the hill. He wondered if the troublesome mutt was still there, and the Beast. The Beast would make an excellent fourth minion.

CHAPTER 14

The Mall

Nat and Sandy entered the layer-cake-shaped West-lake Center Mall on the ground floor.

"The food court is upstairs," Sandy said. "They have a place called Bombay Burritos run by an Indian guy and his Mexican wife. Do you like Indian food?"

Nat grinned and followed Sandy up the escalator, torn pant leg flapping.

Pernicious followed them at a distance in secret. Pernicious was a shape-shifting master of disguise. He tumbled after Nat and Sandy as a windblown wrapper one moment and hitched a ride as a huge wad of gum on someone's shoe the next. He only took his true form when he sensed that no humans were looking. Scuttling atop a platform at the bottom of the escalator, he morphed to blend with a piece of sculpture. An old lady with a cane stepped onto the escalator, her dress dangling perilously near him.

Sandy and Nat rode up. "It looked like the painter of the pictures in your house was a lonely, tortured soul," Sandy said.

"I'm trying to avoid that fate," Nat said.

"Why? Are you a painter?"

"No. But I know how he felt," Nat said.

They stepped off the escalator just as the old woman behind them lost her balance. She twirled her arms and pitched backward as her dress was sucked into the escalator, where Pernicious had stuck it.

Thump-bump-thump-thumpity-bump!

Oblivious, Nat and Sandy headed for Bombay Burritos.

A nearby clothing store caught Pernicious's eye, and he ducked inside. He slunk along a row of dressing rooms, pushing doors open on half-clothed customers, sliding garments off hooks, and scattering pins under bare feet.

In the food court, Sandy and Nat found a seat.

"I've never had a boy take me to dinner on the first date," Sandy said.

"I've never really been on a first date," Nat said.

"That's funny."

"Why?" Nat cringed.

"Because," she said, "me neither, not really."

"My guardian never let me," Nat said.

"Guardian?"

"My parents disappeared in a freak storm when I was twelve."

"Oh. I'm so sorry," Sandy said. "Where'd you go?"

"Different places. Places I didn't like. It's okay, though; they didn't seem to like me much either. I wasn't like other kids." Nat looked away over the balcony. "Looks like some paramedics are helping an old lady down there."

"What about now?" Sandy changed the subject.

"My mentor found me at the state child placement agency. He was training me as an apprentice until a month ago."

"Home school?"

"Something like that."

"How come I haven't seen you at the library until just recently?"

Nat shifted, uncomfortable. "It's been an intense training."

"So what do you do?"

"Does it matter?"

"Just curious. I mean, how do you get by? You're my age."

"I have everything I need, except . . ."

"Except what?"

"I dunno. Trips to the mall with a friend, for instance."

Sandy blushed. "Really, though, what do you do? Now it's killing me."

"I'm sort of a curator."

"Me too! I mean, I'm training to archive books. But then, you knew that. What sort of curator? Museum?"

"No."

"Antiques? Those wonderful things in your house?"

"Look," Nat snapped, "I can't tell you."

"Sorry." Sandy retreated into her food.

Nat slapped his forehead while she was looking down. *I'm an idiot,* he thought. He tried to fix it. "I *can* tell you that I'm supposed to give it all of my concentration all of the time. My mentor must have lectured me a zillion times about how if I missed one single chore, it would be . . ."

". . . the end of the world?" Sandy said.

"Exactly!" Nat exclaimed.

"Sounds just like my parents."

"He was always nagging about duty and responsibility."

Sandy leaned in close, grinned, and whispered, "Well, you're not on duty tonight, and the world doesn't seem to be coming to an end, now does it?"

CHAPTER 15

Burglars

Gus and Richie skateboarded down Nat's dim street. Without streetlights, their dark clothes made them nearly invisible. That was fine with Gus, who wove lazily back and forth, checking car door handles as he went.

He skated over to Neebor's beaten old Chevy and spun to a stop, then hunched down and peered in the window, more out of curiosity than hope that he would find something good to steal. Gus called such cars *c.o.w.s*, which stood for "crap on wheels."

"Moooo!" Gus laughed back at Richie, who had pulled up behind him. "Serious c.o.w. here, dude."

"C'mon, man," said Richie, "the old guy will see us. Let's bust down the hill and see what's going down around downtown."

Gus shook his head, pulled a screwdriver out of his pants pocket, and put a quick scratch in Neebor's car door in the shape of a G. Then he turned to Nat's house. Something caught his eye. He stared for a moment. It would come to him.

"C'mon . . . ," urged Richie.

"Wait, dude," Gus said. "I got a feelin' about somethin'." Then he saw it—the ground-floor window to the study was partially open. Gus grinned. "Hello . . ."

• • •

Richie slid in through the window after Gus, who was already inside puzzling over the ash urns. Their skateboards were tucked in the bushes outside.

Gus went to the mantel of former Keepers and selected an urn. "What the nutty fudge are these things?"

Richie wandered up behind him. "I think they're . . ."

But Gus had already stuck a finger in. He stirred the ashes, then popped his finger into his mouth to taste-test the gray powder.

". . . dead people's ashes," Richie finished.

Gus spat on the floor.

Richie shook his head. "You shouldn't mess with them. Bad karma."

Gus ignored him and grabbed Yatabe the Wanderer's urn. "If it weren't for bad karma, I'd have no karma at all." Gus's laughter rose to its high-pitched giggle as he opened the urn and dumped it upside down. But nothing came out. "This one's empty," Gus complained.

"Hey, man," persisted Richie, "we shouldn't be doing this. There's nothing but old stuff anyway. Let's get out of here."

Gus placed Yatabe's vacant urn back on the shelf with the lid ajar. "C'mon, you wussy, can't hurt to check a couple more rooms."

Before Richie could say another word, Gus was out through the study door and skipping down the dark hallway. Richie took one last look back out through the open window into the moonlit night, then he shook his head and followed his friend into the murky depths of the house.

As Gus and Richie slid down the hall, the eyes of the heads on the bench followed them. Behind them, Yatabe's loose urn lid replaced itself. *Scriiitch . . . clink!* Gus and Richie whirled, both crouching like half-baked ninjas, but they couldn't place the sound. Their eyes darted about.

"It's nuthin'," Gus snapped.

"You go ahead," Richie said. He grabbed the nearest

object, Nat's ornate puzzle box. "I'm gonna just stay and check this out."

"Whatever, dude," Gus said, and he walked deeper into the house, his footsteps echoing through the floor down into the basement.

CHAPTER 16

Something Smells Good

The scent of vagabond boys drifted down to the Beast. It could smell its natural prey now. There were two of them. The Beast listened as they began blundering about in the house above, tantalizing but unreachable. The smell was maddening.

The Beast lumbered over to the feeding chute and began to climb, claw over claw, up the metal frame. The climb was difficult, even with such powerful limbs. There were few handholds on the slick metal besides the ones it had made for itself over the years, dents and deep scratches. The Beast dragged itself upward bit by bit, but the trapdoor at the top was locked tight, as always. It grunted and shimmied back down to the dirt floor far, far below, where it paced and salivated.

The Beast had a vague sense that this was an opportunity but did not know why. It dropped onto all of its six limbs and loped, ape-like, around the perimeter of the deep, dark room, hoping in its simple way to hear the clack of a dead bolt being thrown back on the iron door at the top of the stairs. Long ago, that same bolt had been thrown shut to lock it in this bare prison. The door had always been an impenetrable barrier, but now something was happening on the other side of that door. The Beast crept to the worn stone stairway cut from the raw rock of the wall itself and listened, waiting for the sound and preparing to ascend the long, steep steps to the iron door.

CHAPTER 17

Exploring

Gus walked down the hallway, frowning at the decor. The paintings on the walls frowned back at him. Their pain was so real that Gus wondered what sort of horrors the artist must have seen to paint such things. He tried to laugh, but his laughter echoed in the dark house in a way that he didn't like. "Heh heh, just an old house," he told himself. But he was spooked.

Gus hadn't seen much worth taking. He reached up to touch a grotesque wooden mask. Just as he did, heavy footfalls thumped down the hall.

"Richie . . . ?" he called out. "Is that you, butt breath?"

There was no answer, but a flapping sound came down the hall from the other direction. Gus whirled, wide-eyed, and backed down the hall. He was no wussy, but the strange sounds freaked him out a little. It didn't help that Richie had wimped out. Suddenly, he fell over a large object. *Whump!*

He landed on his back and glanced about frantically, then saw that he'd fallen over a large dog. Gus rolled his eyes, relieved. "You the one been makin' noise?" He scrambled to his feet and gave Bel an unkind kick. "Jeez, I *am* being as big a wussy as Richie." He laughed.

• • •

Richie walked around the study, absently twisting the lid on the puzzle box and waiting for Gus or the sound of the kid or his parents coming home. The house made the hairs on the back of his neck stand up, and he figured that he could make a wussiless exit at the first sign of either one.

Then he found the book on a pedestal. He liked books, and this one looked very cool. He put the puzzle box down and stepped up to the large, leather-bound journal. He opened it near the beginning. There were strange languages and a series of crude drawings showing a person among monsters, either fighting them or friendly with them, he couldn't tell which. He picked up the book and began to look through it.

Behind him, Nik reached out of the puzzle box and pulled himself free, fully visible. Nik blinked, wondering where Nat had gone and who this human boy was, then he heard Gus open the feeding room door, and he tore off to investigate.

CHAPTER 18

Chaos in the Food Court

As Nat and Sandy ate, smiling at each other, the hair on Nat's neck suddenly stood up.

Just then, Pernicious darted under a table nearby. *Oh no!* Nat thought. *How'd he get here?* He had to distract Sandy so that he could nab Pernicious and tuck him away before he did anything malicious.

Nat pointed across the food court at nothing over Sandy's shoulder. "Wow, would you look at that?"

When Sandy turned, Nat whispered fiercely at Pernicious, "Come here!" He pointed at his pocket, but Pernicious scurried away, too excited to be loose in public to cooperate.

Sandy turned to look the direction Nat had pointed, and she accidentally met the eyes of a stunning, perfectly made-up sixteen-year-old girl coming toward them. "Uh-oh." Sandy frowned. "Chelsea Wallace."

The head of every teen boy in the food court rotated as Chelsea wiggled past with two just slightly less-glamorous female lackeys in tow.

"Look, you guys." Chelsea smirked to her friends. "It's the little librarian out on the town." She paused next to Sandy's table. "Hey, Sandy Nerdz, is this your boyfriend or your cousin or both?"

Chelsea's lackeys giggled.

"Come on, Nat," Sandy said, "we should go."

But Nat was still looking for Pernicious. He spotted the little demon scuttling behind Chelsea, disguised as a floor tile. "Pernicious!" he hissed.

Chelsea frowned. "What's that supposed to mean?"

Nat looked up, bewildered.

One of Chelsea's friends said, "It means you think you're too cool."

"No, I think it means you're a tramp," said the other.

Sandy couldn't help but grin. " 'Pretentious' and 'promiscuous,' " she said. "Great guesses, but 'pernicious' actually means you're trying to cause trouble."

"Thanks, Random House," said Chelsea, "but when I need an encyclopedia . . ."

"Thesaurus," corrected Sandy.

". . . I'll page you." Chelsea turned her heavily mascaraed gaze on Nat. "Hey, freaky new guy," she sneered, loud enough to ensure that every teen in the food court turned to watch, "you know what I think . . . ?"

Chelsea took one step back, enjoying her huge audience, and she planted her high heel right on Pernicious. It knocked the wind from him, forcing out the longest, wettest demonic grunt imaginable.

Plllbbbbbbbt!

Chelsea froze. Her face went white as her entire social life flashed before her eyes. Kids stared, but nobody saw Pernicious. They saw only Chelsea and heard only the sound of a tremendous fart. They began to giggle privately, then louder and louder, joining in a great, growing chorus of laughter. Even Chelsea's two sidekicks were snickering.

Amidst the chaos, Nat saw his chance to leap on Pernicious. Nat grabbed him and stuffed him in his pocket without being spotted. Everyone else was watching Chelsea, who was halfway across the food court by now. Experienced in her high heels, she was able to run very fast.

When Nat stood up, mall security was there, and they were not happy with the hubbub. "You two seem to be in the middle of all this," said a skinny officer. "I think I'd better escort you out."

"I'm sorry," Nat said to Sandy as the guard walked them toward the escalator. "I didn't mean to ruin your evening."

Sandy looked conflicted, as though she might laugh or cry or both at the same time. "I don't know what you did or how you did it," she said, "but you don't have to apologize for sticking up for me."

CHAPTER 19

Don't Go in the Basement

Gus stood in front of the trough in the bathroom with his pants down. Nik snuck in beneath him and crouched under the tub, scowling at Gus's use of it. He slipped from the shadows, sniffing around Gus's feet. He eyed Gus's shoelaces, grinned, then reached for them.

Gus ran both hands through his greasy hair, oblivious, shaking his hips and daredevil whizzing with no hands.

"You know, you're right, Richie!" Gus yelled. "There ain't nothin' good to take in this house. No laptop, no TV, no Xbox. Might as well get goin' when I'm done here."

Beneath Gus, Nik was hoisting a mop handle. He cocked it back like he was casting a fishing pole, then delivered a vicious blow.

Thud!

Gus felt something slam into his most sensitive parts.

He squealed and scrambled backward, staring down in horror. He saw a squat, ghastly creature with nasty teeth lurking under the trough. It held a mop, which it cocked back for another swing.

Gus staggered to the door and stumbled into the hall, gasping for breath, but somehow his feet got tangled. He went to the ground, hard.

Whump!

He groaned, struggled to his feet, and began to waddle madly down the hall as he hoisted up his pants. Two steps later, he went down again.

Whump!

Gus crawled down the hall, dazed, certain that the little creature would stomp up his back to take a bite out of his neck. He couldn't stand up. He looked down. His shoelaces were tied together.

He kicked off his shoes and scrambled down the hall, skidding across the foyer to the front door. He slid a dead bolt back and tried to open it. It was still locked.

"What the . . . ?"

Gus rattled the knob and pounded on the door. Sounds rose behind him, coming down the hall—growling, flapping, and heavy footfalls. It was definitely not Richie. Gus looked around, frantic. Then he spotted the heavy iron basement door. The huge Indian rug shifted under Gus's feet. He yelped and dove for the basement door, clawing at its heavy bolts and throwing them back one after the other.

After the last bolt, Gus pulled at the door. It didn't budge at first. He groaned, thinking that the door was stuck. Then it began to move, slowly, with the painful squeal of iron on stone. Gus threw everything he had into a desperate shove, and the four-inch-thick iron slab finally moved enough for him to slip past and escape the foyer.

The light filtered through the narrow opening and fell on stone stairs leading down into total darkness. Gus didn't have time to check it out. He plunged through, turned, and pulled with his full weight, struggling and yanking until the door swung slowly toward him. Finally, it shut with a *clang* that sounded through the entire basement.

CHAPTER 20

The Basement Door

Nikolai thumped up to the basement door, and Flappy made an unsteady landing on Nik's thick head. They stared, motionless, like two stone gargoyles. Their expressions of mischievous glee vanished as the unlocked iron door loomed over them, not funny at all.

Nik was brave by nature, but even he would move no closer. Atop his head, Flappy uttered cautionary little coo-gurgles through his hooked beak. Nik began to tiptoe backward.

They were both about to slink away when, suddenly, the other human boy arrived in the foyer.

• • •

Richie stumbled from the hallway into the foyer. He froze, staring at the two little demons, the *DK Journal* tucked under one arm and his backpack slung over the other shoulder. The demons turned and stared back. For a moment Richie was puzzled. The misshapen things on the floor looked like statues. Then Flappy cocked his head, parrot-like.

Richie's puzzlement was replaced by pure disbelief. He shook his head, hoping to clear his mind of what he thought he saw. But even after he blinked, the impossible little creatures were still there. In fact, Nik was bending left and right, trying to get a better look at him. *They're real,* Richie thought, *and they're alive.*

He heard distant, scraping footfalls begin beyond the iron door, deep in the basement. The steps were heavy, powerful.

The little demons stiffened and stepped in place nervously, stuck between the door and Richie, unable to decide which way to scatter.

The footsteps from below grew faster, moving eagerly up the stairs. Richie saw that the bolts on the iron door hung open. Things were getting weird. He turned to flee.

Then he heard something that kept him there. "What the hell?" barked a muffled voice behind the iron door. Richie sucked in a breath. It was Gus.

A low, menacing growl rose up the stairs. There was a human yelp of surprise, then a sickening thud. Gasps and violent thumps followed, the unmistakable sounds of a struggle.

Nik and Flappy were as petrified as Richie. All three of them stared at the door, a private audience for the concert of desperate noises beyond, until . . .

Suddenly, the door flew open and Gus dove halfway out, onto his belly. His face contorted in agony. He struggled to crawl into the foyer. His shirt was torn to red-stained ribbons. He looked up at Richie with pleading eyes and thrust a hand out to him.

Richie took an involuntary step toward Gus to help. Too late. Something yanked Gus back through the doorway. He disappeared into the darkness, and the heavy iron door swung almost shut. There was a horrible ripping sound.

Then there was silence.

Richie exhaled. "Gus . . . ?"

Richie started toward the door, but it moved again, and he froze. The massive iron door began to squeal open. Darkness trickled out. A huge claw emerged from the shadows behind the door and gripped its edge. Another claw appeared, then another, then another. The furry hands felt along the door for handholds and shoved the heavy iron thing outward with an ease that belied brute strength.

Richie's eyes went saucer size. It was definitely *not* Gus.

CHAPTER 21

Good-Night Kiss?

Nat felt strange riding in a car with a girl his age driving. Dhaliwahl didn't drive, so Nat hadn't been in any sort of car for years. She seemed a very careful driver—not a *good* driver, but extremely cautious. It was obvious she was new at it. She pulled up to Nat's curb and began her parallel-parking routine. Back and forth, back and forth, back and forth, until the car was poorly aligned to her satisfaction. Nat wondered at her persistence and marveled at her lack of skill.

Sandy turned the key, and the car shuddered. She winced, then chuckled. "This has been an odd evening," she said. "I still can't decide whether I'm incredibly entertained or totally mortified. I've certainly never been kicked out of anyplace before."

Nat smiled back weakly, wondering if smiling was the

right thing to do. "I really am sorry," he said. He had an instinct for demons, but he had no instinct for this. He felt a nervous energy that he couldn't control. It urged him to reach out to the female human sitting next to him and yet to run away as fast as possible at the same time. Instead, Nat simply fidgeted. Finally, he reached for the door handle.

Sandy hit the automatic door locks. *Click!* He was trapped.

Sandy took a deep breath. "You know, I'm usually pretty careful. I don't take a lot of risks."

"No?"

"Definitely no. But I think you're, um, interesting. And nice. I don't meet a lot of nice guys . . . any guys, really. So today when you came into the library, I just thought, maybe I should get out from behind my safe little desk and take a chance."

Sandy leaned toward Nat, putting her hand on his arm. Suddenly, the hairs on the back of his neck shot up as though a powerful demon had just been unleashed. He searched Sandy's eyes. She smiled. He reached out and took her chin in his hand. But instead of kissing her, he pushed her lip back with a finger to inspect her teeth. "You're not going to bite me, are you?"

"No . . . ," she mumbled around his prodding finger.

"I, uh, I was just checking the . . . my teacher told

Demonkeeper
87

me there is a type of girl that preys on boys, although usually in their beds."

Sandy pulled away abruptly. She sat up, her hands retreating to the steering wheel. Nat realized that he'd said something terribly wrong.

Sandy stared straight ahead and spoke tersely to the windshield. "I don't think I'm *that* kind of a girl, Nathaniel. In fact, maybe this whole thing *was* a mistake. Why don't we just shake hands and call it a night."

Nat wasn't sure what he'd done, but he knew it was *not* good. And she definitely wasn't a succubus. "Okay," he said softly. He extended his hand.

Although Sandy had offered to shake, she didn't really seem to want to. But his hand looked a bit ridiculous dangling there in midair by itself, so she reached out and shook it without looking at him. She wasn't smiling anymore.

"Good night," tried Nat, mustering a final attempt at a half smile.

Sandy didn't answer but simply released his automatic door lock. *Clack!*

CHAPTER 22

The Beast

Richie stared in horror at the basement door as the huge claws pushed it outward. Nik and Flappy were able to take one step back before a clawed fist erupted from the darkness and slammed down on the fir floor. The little demons scattered as the blow crunched the wood where they'd been sitting only a split second earlier. Six massive claws flailed after them. Nik and Flappy darted for the puzzle box. A huge, multi-armed shadow leapt after them, thumping across the floor. Just as a thick claw swiped for Flappy's tail, the two minions dove at the box and were sucked inside through the small hole in the top. The claw missed them but whapped the box viciously across the room.

The thing stopped and sniffed the air. It smelled something. . . .

Richie leapt from his hiding place behind the door and swung Sandy's flowerpot desperately at the back of its thick head.

Crash!

Four stump-like legs whirled as the creature, unfazed by the blow, turned to face Richie, and he got a good look at the Beast for the first time. It loomed over him like a great hulking gorilla with multiple rows of razor teeth and curved claws. Its six hairy limbs were neither legs nor arms, but some grotesque combination of the two. Its beady yellow eyes lit up when it saw Richie, and it eased open its tooth-lined mouth wider than its entire head, like a snake unhinging its jaw to devour a mouse.

Richie closed his eyes. A little street kid didn't stand much chance against something so powerful, something with such an obvious, drooling, insatiable hunger.

Then Richie remembered a line from a book he'd read called *The Underbed Goblin: When it comes to monsters, a boy's refuge is beneath his blanket.* He crouched and grabbed the Indian rug, meaning to pull it over himself. It made no sense, really, and he didn't know how it might help, but somehow it seemed the right thing to do. The Beast lunged forward, aiming an outstretched claw at Richie's ducking head. But just then, the rug wiggled to life in Richie's hands. It also wriggled to life beneath the multiple feet of the Beast.

The creature fought for balance and went down. *Whump!* It landed no more than six inches from Richie's nose. Its great bulk shook the floor. The rug jerked out of Richie's hands and wrapped itself around the giant Beast. Bending and stretching, the rug held the flailing monster. The Beast struggled to regain its feet, but its great strength worked against it as the rug curled, shifted, and slid, keeping it off balance.

Richie grabbed the *DK Journal* and raised the heavy book to hit the Beast should it break free from the rug. But he saw that the two creatures were fully engaged. He leapt past them, ran down the hall with the *DK Journal* under one arm, reached the study on a dead sprint, and dove out through the open window into the night.

• • •

Back in the foyer, there was a great rending sound that could have been flesh or cloth. The rug fell away, limp and defeated, and the hunched shadow of the Beast rose on the wall.

The thing rubbed its sore head and tromped to the backpack Richie had left behind. It lowered its wet snout to sniff it. The pack smelled of misplaced boy. The Beast crouched there for a moment, breathing it in, enjoying the aroma, committing it to memory. Then the massive creature grunted and stomped off in the direction that Richie had run, nose to the ground, bloodhound style.

CHAPTER 23

A Bad End to a Bad Day

Nat walked up to his porch. When it shuddered under his foot, he shook his head and went around the house to the back door, too tired for more foolishness.

Inside, he walked past the foyer without even giving it a look and headed up to his bedroom, leaving behind him the scattered remnants of the wild things that had happened there only moments earlier.

Nat entered his bedroom, pulled Pernicious from his pocket by the scruff of the neck, and dropped him on the floor. He halfheartedly motioned the comforter on his bed aside. Going to bed seemed a good idea. He could cut his losses on a very bad day. Tomorrow he could wake up and pretend that the disastrous date had never happened. He decided that he would avoid the library for a while, maybe forever.

His heavy comforter was ancient and stitched with rich purples and golds. The gold threads actually *were* gold. The cloth had been sewn for a royal ambassador of the Song Empire in southern China during the 1200s. The comforter fluttered aside for him, revealing Bel, who was hiding underneath the bed. Nat bent down.

"Hey, Bel, what's going on, boy?"

Bel whimpered.

Nat's foggy head suddenly cleared. Bel was the most laid-back beast Nat had ever known—he never whimpered. Something was wrong.

Nat marched back out into the hall. "What's going on?" he demanded.

The wooden mask began to blabber. "Careful!" it warned.

"Look out!" said the iron mask.

"Can you be more specific?" asked Nat.

"I certainly can," said the wooden mask.

"No, you can't," said Iron.

"You are like an itch I can't scratch," Wood snapped back.

They fell to bickering. Nat moved on.

Something was definitely not right, and when things were not as they should be, the answer was usually . . .

"Flappy? Nik? Did you get out?"

Nat looked in the study, checking under the couch

and behind the bookshelf for the little troublemakers. Then he saw the open window. *Not good,* he thought.

Nat began to close the window. But just as he reached for the latch, he glanced at the nearby pedestal where the *DK Journal* had sat for years. The blood drained from his face. It was gone.

Nat burst from the study and hurried down the hall, examining everything now. The loss of the *Journal* was the worst thing that could possibly happen at the end of the worst day of his short career as a Keeper. At least that's what he thought until he reentered the foyer.

"Oh no . . ."

The vase was in pieces and scattered around the entryway table. The dented puzzle box was on the floor. A backpack with an anarchy symbol lay near the hallway like a discarded rag. And across the foyer, the blood-spattered basement door hung wide open.

CHAPTER 24

What to Do?

Nat finished cleaning the foyer and put the mop back in the bucket of red water. He recognized the backpack. It belonged to one of the two skateboarders he'd seen together at the library. From the amount of blood around the basement door, it was clear there was only one left now.

Nat fought back tears as he wrung out the mop. "I've let the world down, Bel," he said. "I had one job . . . one! Keep demons. Not run off and have 'big fun,' not try a date or two to see what all the fuss is about . . . just keep demons." Nat looked up. "How could I let a girl completely distract me?"

Bel just licked himself.

"Dhaliwahl didn't tell me enough about the Beast."

Nat recalled the few words his mentor had shared about the Beast. . . .

● ● ●

"I am old and need replacing, Nathaniel," Dhaliwahl had said just two short months ago as they stood in the same foyer where Nat stood now. "A pity it took so long to find you after . . ."

"After what?" Nat had asked.

"After my first apprentice did not work out. A piece of the past that is not your concern."

A distant growling rose from the basement.

"Ah, your friend is awake," said Dhaliwahl.

Nat shivered and eyed the basement door. The Beast growled whenever Nat was nearby. "What is its nature?" Nat said.

"Why do you keep asking?" Dhaliwahl frowned.

"Why do you change the subject every time I ask?"

"To know something is not always to feel more at ease," Dhaliwahl grumbled, "but I shall tell you this. It is a demon of the First Order that can touch all five human senses and a mindless eating machine. It can devour a boy in seconds and be hungry again an hour later. And it cannot be controlled, so far as we know. That is why you must keep it trapped in the basement."

"I don't think I can handle a creature like that without you," Nat said.

"You are not expected to handle it, just keep it. Yatabe the Wanderer tried to handle it long ago when it was captured."

"Yatabe?"

"Yes. He had been one of our order's most revered members." Dhaliwahl sighed. The memory was painful for him.

"What happened?" Nat asked.

"He was dis . . . membered."

Nat squirmed. He knew Dhaliwahl's mentor had been devoured by a First Order demon. There had been no remains to put in Yatabe's jar. But Nat didn't know that the demon was the Beast in his own basement.

"Tell me more," he begged.

"I will tell you but one thing more," Dhaliwahl offered. "It will track its natural prey relentlessly."

"What is its natural prey?"

"One thing more is not two things more."

"But how was it captured?" Nat tried to sneak in yet another question.

"With great courage," Dhaliwahl snapped back.

"That's not an answer."

"Ah, but the answers are in here"—Dhaliwahl gestured at the *DK Journal*—"and here." Dhaliwahl's blind finger found Nat's heart.

• • •

"I must go after it," Nat said to himself. He wasn't sure exactly what he meant to go after—the *Journal* or the Beast. Recovering the *Journal* was possible, but capturing the Beast? Only an experienced Keeper could hope to survive such a mission, let alone accomplish it. His minions could come with him in the puzzle box, but he would need more help.

Nat went to the Demonkeeper's cabinet and opened the door. There was only one Demonkeeper's tool he knew of that was powerful enough to be of use against the Beast—Dhaliwahl's snake staff. He didn't know how to use it yet, but extreme times called for extreme measures.

Nat dug in the cabinet and found what he was looking for—a small, ornate case snuggled in the corner. Inside the case was a coil of rope. Nat pulled the rope out of the closet carefully by its tail. Suddenly, it writhed and reared up, its bobbing cobra head as alive as any pit viper's in the jungles of India. Nat hurriedly snapped it like a whip. It straightened, stiffening into Dhaliwahl's staff.

Nat sighed heavily, relieved that it hadn't killed him immediately. After taking a moment to make sure that the snake would hold its shape, he raised it to his eye and examined its lines as though choosing a cue at the pool hall.

Staff in hand, Nat motioned to the injured rug. "Are you with me?" It rolled itself out for him. He waved at the clock. "It is time for you to cooperate. How say you?" The clock hands spun and landed on midnight. Nat nodded approvingly. He whirled and pointed the staff dramatically at the nearby wooden lamp responsible for the flickering light in the room. "And you, erratic giver of light, will you brighten a path for your Keeper?" The lamp stopped flickering and shined its light on Nat as though he were a rock star.

Nat pumped his fist. "Yes!" They were listening to him. Emboldened, he held the snake staff up like a shaman and tried to deepen his voice. "Hear me, all creatures of this house, for I am Nathaniel Grimlock, Keeper of . . . !"

He was about to say "demons" when the staff went limp. The light flickered and lit his rump clownishly. The clock stopped. Nathaniel stepped back and tripped over the carpet, falling flat on his butt.

CHAPTER 25

Window Shopping

The Thin Man stood over a huge claw print in the dirt in Neebor's garden. His minions looked on from his pockets and shoulders.

"The Beassst"—he grinned—"it'sss loossse."

He eyed the window of Nat's house. A single lamp burned on the first floor, outlining a silhouette of Nat with his arms in the air.

"Ah, and there isss Dhaliwahl'sss new apprentisss. How quaint."

The Thin Man watched, absently barbecuing Neebor's flower petals with Charr, who danced at his fingertip. "I could challenge him now." He cocked his bony head and smiled at the thought. "But he may know how to find the Beassst. We'll follow him. Yesss. He will lead usss ssstraight to it if he isss a ssskilled Keeper."

Then the lamp inside the house flickered, and the silhouette of Nat fell over backward.

Thump!

CHAPTER 26

The Streets Aren't Safe

Richie rolled down the alley on his skateboard. The shadows seemed to reach out to him, beckoning. His eyes darted about as his board clattered over the cracked pavement.

The back alleys of Seattle were his world, but he didn't feel comfortable in them now. There were no friends around. There were no cops either, for that matter. For once in his life, he would have felt better if there were. And his best friend had just been . . . He didn't want to think about it.

Richie jumped at a sudden noise and kicked his board up into his hands. He saw nothing in the alley, but that was exactly the problem. Something had made a noise, yet there was nothing there. He began to walk away. He had read a book called *Animal Action* that described how predators stalked their prey until their prey began to sense danger, then they sprang. Richie's walk turned into a trot. Before he knew it, he was running down the alley and out into the open street as fast as his legs could carry him.

Moments later, a huge, hunched shadow fell across the alley, snuffling along the track Richie left behind.

CHAPTER 27
A Reluctant Ally

Sandy sat at the front desk. The sun was just peeking through the east window on its way up. Early on Sunday, the library was empty. Sandy relished these times, because she could catch up on her homework, or sit and read, or just think. It was peaceful.

Liz hated it. Called it boring.

"You went out to dinner?" Liz laughed. "With Captain Creepy? Good God, Sandra Nertz, I was kidding when I suggested you should be anywhere near that freak outside the safety of this building."

Sandy sorted books, weathering the ridicule. She deserved it, she thought. The date had been a disaster.

Liz continued. "I mean, c'mon, the guy is into embalming."

Demonkeeper

"Cremation," Sandy corrected her.

"Oh yeah, right," Liz said. "That's completely different."

"He just seemed intriguing. I thought it might be . . ." Sandy looked off into the distance. ". . . an adventure."

"An adventure?" Liz struggled to hold back another laugh.

"I guess I was wrong." Sandy sighed.

Just then, someone banged through the front door. Both girls looked up and saw Nat stumble into the lobby. His hair was disheveled. His eyes were bloodshot.

"Whoa," Liz said, "speak of the devil worshiper."

Nat hurried to the reference desk. "I need your help!"

"Whatever it is," Liz said, "I'm sure we don't have it, not even in our special 'death-related hobbies' section." Liz stepped in front of Sandy protectively and folded her arms.

"C'mon, please," pleaded Nat. "I need to find the street kid, one of the boys with the skateboards that come in here sometimes."

Sandy looked out from behind Liz. "You're not looking for a book?"

"No. Well, yes. But first for the kid."

"Green hair?"

Nat's stomach lurched at the memory of the green-haired kid whose blood he'd washed from his foyer. "No, the other one," he said.

"That's Richie. Why?"

Nat paused, unsure how much he wanted to tell her. "He broke into my home," he said finally.

Sandy gasped. "Are you sure?"

Liz smirked. "That's him, all right."

Nat dug in his tote bag. He pulled out Richie's backpack.

Sandy recognized the pack. "Oh no!" she cried. "He'll go to juvy."

"Good," Liz said, and wandered off.

"Nathaniel, Richie likes to read," Sandy said. "He's bright. He's got a chance. I'll bet that little jerk Gus got him into this."

"Listen, I'm not looking to get him into more trouble. But he's got something important of mine. If you help me find him, I'd be happy to keep the police out of it."

"He's probably hanging out around Pike Place Market or Pioneer Square."

"Can you take me to look for him?" Nat said.

"Why me?"

"Because I realized that you have something important that I don't."

"What?"

Demonkeeper

"A car."

Moments later, Liz turned to see Nat hustle out of the library. She went back to the reference desk, curious. "You certainly sent Satan's little helper packing. I'm proud of you, for once."

Sandy closed her purse, grabbed her car keys, and stepped out from behind the desk. "Can you cover for me?"

"Sure, I . . . Wait, where are you going?"

"To help keep a kid out of jail." Sandy trotted to the exit.

Liz stared after her, shaking her head. "What's gotten into her?" she mumbled as she picked U.G.G. up off the floor and put it back on the shelf.

• • •

Nat could feel Sandy's aura radiating from the old Volvo. The car was cautious, practical, and square. He rattled the handle. The door was locked tight.

Nearby, a man in a trench coat held up a newspaper, hiding his face. As Nat fussed with Sandy's door, a small hole burned through the sports page. The black eye of the Thin Man peeked through, watching him.

Sandy arrived at the car. "What did he take, anyway?" she asked.

Nat debated whether to tell her for a moment. "A journal," he said finally.

"A book?" Sandy unlocked her own door, but she didn't let Nat in.

"A journal." Nat tried the handle. "An antique passed down from, uh, person to person for about"—he paused—"for a long time."

Sandy grew even more curious. "As in generations? Centuries?"

Nat frowned, impatient. They had to get moving. "Oh, nuh-nuh-no." He shook his head, motioning for her to let him into the car. "Much longer than that."

Sandy's eyebrows arched, and she unlocked Nat's door. Nat piled in, and Sandy carefully maneuvered the car out into the street.

As the Volvo sputtered away, the Thin Man lowered the paper. His pencil-thin eyebrows arched. "The *Demonkeeper Journal* isss in the handsss of a mere boy?!"

CHAPTER 28

Sneakers

A droopy kid sat on the bustling corner at Pike and Second Avenue, begging change from pedestrians. He thanked them for pity coins with a nod and insulted their mothers when rejected. With his ragged shirt and big eyes he did a brisk little business with the strangers who didn't recognize him. But those who frequented Pike Place Market knew that this boy who looked poor had hundred-dollar tennis shoes in his backpack. After a day of begging, he'd put on his shiny shoes, count his loot, and grin ear to ear.

As the boy swung his gloomy, practiced expression from one passerby to the next, he heard a familiar voice.

"Sneakers!" Richie approached and held up a high five.

Seeing Richie, Sneakers threw off his basset hound expression and smiled.

"Hey, Richie, you want to sit with me for a bit?" Sneakers said. "We can pretend we're orphan brothers."

"I *am* an orphan," said Richie.

"Yeah, but we're not brothers." Sneakers laughed. Sneakers had a habit of laughing at things that weren't funny.

"You're on your own, dude," Richie said. "I gotta keep cruising today."

"Police lookin' for ya?"

"Nah. But I got a feeling like I should be a moving target just the same."

"Know what you mean." Sneakers grinned. "Later days, my friend."

"Later."

It felt bad walking away from a solid companion, but somehow Richie felt it might be worse if he stayed.

• • •

A few minutes after Richie's visit, Sneakers packed it in. He folded up his basket and dropped his cardboard Spare Change sign into his backpack. Business was slowing. There were other corners where he would be a fresh face to a different crowd. He fished his bright white tennis shoes out of his backpack and switched them for his ratty sandals with holes in the soles.

Demonkeeper

Nearby, down a shadowy alley, a football-sized section of pavement bulged upward. It rose from the very ground, morphing into a sloping asphalt skull. Yellow eyes appeared in it. They blinked once as the bulge continued to grow up from the street, and they glared down the alley, zeroing in on Sneakers.

Sneakers almost passed the alley without going in. But his habit was too strong. He needed a cigarette. He ducked into the alley and rummaged in his pocket for his pack of smokes.

The Beast writhed, almost free of the pavement. Its snout rotated in the direction of Sneakers's thin trail of stinky cigarette smoke as it pulled its massive paws loose from the asphalt.

Sneakers hadn't even taken a drag on his cigarette yet. He was just holding it, enjoying the mysterious twists of the white wisps that curled up from the smoldering tip. He raised the cigarette to his lips, about to take his first puff, and *Wham!* The Beast drove into him like a compact freight train and knocked him through the air. By some miracle, Sneakers landed on his feet and hit the pavement running. He didn't even know what had smashed into him, but it was big, it was growling, and it was right behind him. He fled deeper into the alley.

The chase was short. A couple years of cigarettes had already done him some disservice. Sneakers wheezed

and stumbled. As he ran, he made the mistake of looking back, and his white tennis shoe caught on a bump in
the pavement. He felt his world shift beneath him, and
the sky traded places with the ground.

Whump!

Sneakers hit the cement and tumbled to a stop. There
was an awful moment when he knew that the thing would
catch him now. He could hear its heavy panting.

But when he flipped around, nothing was there. A
wave of relief swept through him. Sneakers propped
himself up on his elbows. For a moment, he thought
he would be okay. Then the street began to shift before
his eyes. The pavement rose up, taking shape, growing, morphing. There were hulking legs, powerful arms,
long, yellow claws, and before Sneakers could think to
scramble away, the Beast had arrived. It stood over him,
its rows of gleaming teeth smiling at him from between
black lips.

CHAPTER 29

Nat and Sandy Split Up

Nat leapt out of Sandy's car, stuffing the snake staff in his jacket. He rushed to the edge of a nearby skate park, where he saw three street kids on skateboards. None of them were Richie. Sandy arrived behind him at the edge of the skate bowl.

"Now what?" Nat exclaimed. "Now what?!"

"Now nothing," Sandy said. "I've driven every north-south street from Elliott Bay to Capitol Hill in numerical order. We've surveyed every homeless shelter I've ever taken used books to. This is our last stop, unless you want to start walking dark alleys."

Nat paused to consider her suggestion.

"I was kidding!" barked Sandy, horrified.

The kids in the skate bowl began to give them dirty looks, so they walked away. A half block later, Nat spotted a concrete bench. He started kicking it repeatedly and painfully.

"Nathaniel, stop," Sandy said. He kept kicking. "Nathaniel!" She grabbed him.

Nat whirled, desperate and frantic. "What?!"

Sandy stepped back. "It's okay. You can just . . . I mean, street kids usually turn up eventually."

"No, it's not okay! It's definitely not okay. Oh, man! This is all my fault."

"Your fault?"

"I never should have gone out with you last night."

Sandy winced.

Nat continued. "I just got this job, and the first chance I get, I blow it!" Nat dropped his head into his hands. "He trusted me."

"Who?" Sandy said softly, hoping to calm Nat down. She didn't understand everything he was saying.

Nat looked up suddenly. "Wait. We've been completely methodical. I'm so stupid! We'll never find him that way. Chaos doesn't follow street numbers." He pointed with his staff to what looked like the creepiest alley in all of Seattle. "Maybe if we just start wandering around . . ."

Sandy shook her head. "Oh no. I have a normal, safe life that I value, Nathaniel. I do *not* wander deserted alleys at night."

Demonkeeper

"You don't have to," said Nat, "I do."

He looked so sad and sincere that Sandy instantly felt bad for barking at him. "You don't even have a way to get home."

"Nonsense, I just walk that way a couple of miles." Nat thrust a finger west without looking, then saw he was pointing out into Elliott Bay. He moved his finger vaguely north instead.

There was no talking sense to him, so Sandy gave up. "Fine." She shook her head. "I'm leaving you here."

Nat nodded and began to walk away.

Sandy yelled after him, "I've got plenty of other things to do tonight anyway!"

CHAPTER 30

The Skate Park

The sign at the skate park read SKATE AT YOUR OWN RISK.

Skip, Dexter and Mags stood atop the skate bowl, prepping for another run. They'd been interrupted by the staring kid with the weird snake stick and the girl with him, but now they had the place to themselves again.

They pretty much owned the park. Mags and Skip pitched camp twenty feet away in an abandoned bus shelter with some other kids every night. Dex didn't live in the shelter—he had a home a mile east and parents who wished he'd stay there. He just dropped by every day to skate.

Mags, a freckled but tough-looking teen girl, was picking her line. "Figure eight, and you bomb down the middle after my first cut." She motioned for Skip to follow her as she leapt out into space on her board. The concrete dropped away, her board gained speed, and Mags shot across the trough.

Skip watched and waited, timing his run. When Mags rode up the right side of the bowl and turned, he dove straight down the middle.

His run was faster than he or Mags had planned. Moments later his hurtling body met hers at the far end of the bowl with a meaty *smack*. Skip went down, bouncing across the pavement. Mags winced but rode through it. She turned and weaved her way back up to the rim, where Dexter stood laughing.

"Pancake!" Dex shouted. Indeed, Skip was sprawled flat on his stomach.

Mags kicked her board up into her hands. "Weak, man." She frowned. "I almost lost my momentum."

A bulge in the nearby sidewalk moved toward them like the dorsal fin of a shark hidden just below the surface of the pavement. Dexter felt a chill and turned. The thing veered toward him, somehow slicing through the concrete without cracking it. Dexter leapt aside, and it rushed past him.

"What was that?" he yelped.

Mags saw it and watched it go. "I dunno," she said, "but it almost slammed you." She chuckled at first, but the bulge curled over the lip of the bowl and surged down the wall toward Skip's prone form. Her smile disappeared. "It's heading for Skip," she said.

"Skip, look out!" Dexter yelled. Skip only groaned and held up his middle finger.

Mags launched herself toward Skip, bombing down the wall.

Skip rolled over and saw Mags coming. He braced himself and shot her a bucktoothed, thirteen-year-old grin. "So, you want some more, huh?"

He was still grinning when Mags saw the pavement open up beneath him. The concrete parted like a great mouth lined with jagged concrete teeth. Skip looked surprised, then he dropped into the blackness, and the opening closed around him.

Mags reached out. One moment Skip was there, the next her wheels rolled smoothly over the spot where he had been, and it was as though he had never existed at all.

"Mags, get out of there!" Dexter screamed as he lost sight of her around the corner.

But she couldn't. Her momentum wouldn't carry her up over the lip at the far end. Mags saw that she'd have to spin around and ride through the bowl again to pick up enough velocity. She turned a corner and rode halfway up to the rim, then cut a flawless one-eighty and started back down, hugging the wall.

She tucked tight and leaned hard, but just as she was gaining speed, two huge claws reached out of the wall, and she never made it to the trough.

Dexter saw Mags's empty skateboard roll slowly back into view. There was a jagged, crescent-shaped chunk missing from it. He scanned the skate park for his street friends, but all he saw were Mags's broken skateboard and Skip's tattered baseball cap.

Dexter backed away from the skate park, turned, and fled to the east.

CHAPTER 31

Dark Clouds Gather

Sandy stomped to her car, got in, and slammed the door. "He can find his own way home," she grumbled. But the sad truth was that she did *not* have anything else to do tonight, except maybe clean the cat box. The most excitement she'd had in months was the crazy incident at Westlake Center Mall. The memory of it made her chuckle.

She turned the ignition and jerked away from the curb. The radio came on. The KPLU weatherwoman spoke with the resigned tone of a person weary of forecasting rain day after day.

". . . and so look out, Seattle," she said, "because tonight it's thundershowers for hours and hours."

As the weatherwoman prattled on about Doppler

radars and cold fronts giving way to high- or low-pressure systems, Sandy slumped in her seat and let the guilt sink in. She'd abandoned the only boy who had ever asked her out, and now he was going to get drenched.

CHAPTER 32

Drifting in a Sea of Chaos

Nat picked his way through a busy Pioneer Square crowd. Hundreds of people bustled along the sidewalk, tossing Nat to and fro. When he stepped into the street to avoid them, whizzing cars nearly ran him over.

"Chaos," Nat reminded himself, "embrace it." He found an empty doorway and removed the puzzle box from his inside pocket, where he had tucked it before leaving the house. "Okay, you guys, show me how." He twisted the lid.

His minions squeezed out of the box. Nat stood in the midst of the crowd, but nobody blinked at the appearance of the little demons. Because none of them *saw* the little demons.

Pernicious morphed himself into the scenery. He flattened himself into a shadow and floated after a trotting dog, then ducked under a moving car and emerged from the other side as a tumbling aluminum can and catapulted himself into a bag lady's shopping cart for a free ride across the square.

Nik lost himself in the crowd, blending like a chameleon with his surroundings. He sniffed the ground and shuffled off down the sidewalk, weaving through the packed throng and disappearing in an ocean of swishing legs. The hurried and preoccupied pedestrians didn't dare stop to look down for fear of being trampled, and when the crowd thinned, Nik simply slipped off to a nearby object and molded himself to it in both shape and color.

Flappy wove skyward, and the breeze swallowed him up. He fluttered to and fro, hidden by curtains of overlapping air, drifting invisibly and aimlessly on unseen currents of wind. Even Nat could barely make him out.

They'd been hiding from humans for centuries, and they were good at it, but Nat was still amazed at how they could simply disappear in the wild, like deer in the tall grass.

He wasn't sure that they'd come back, but he didn't follow them. If a homeless boy was cast adrift in the city's sea of uncertainty only to wash up in some dark alley, then riding the current of those same chaotic streets might take Nat there too. He picked a direction at random and began walking.

Richie didn't want to stop moving, but he had to rest. He plopped down on the grate in the sidewalk that pulled warm exhaust from the kitchen of a Thai restaurant. It smelled spicy, peanutty. Richie liked sleeping on this grate. The heavenly smells usually kept bad dreams at bay. He'd been tormented by strange dreams ever since he could remember, but nothing so horrible as what he had witnessed in the house.

He rested his head on the bizarre book he'd found himself clutching when he'd stopped running at the bottom of Queen Anne Hill. The book was both sturdy and soft somehow, reassuring. His head sank into the worn leather cover as though it was the headrest of a safe, comfortable recliner. But even the reassuring *Journal* couldn't hold off the feeling that more bad things were coming and that staying in one place for very long was dangerous.

At that very moment, a long shadow fell across him. Richie's eyes popped open. Too late to run. He hoped the shadow would move past without noticing him.

A smaller shadow circled overhead. *Flappity-flap-flap* . . . The little shadow circled once and moved off, zigzagging back toward a looming silhouette at the opening of the alley.

The long shadow stepped forward. It wasn't a monster. It was the weird kid from the old house.

Nat walked toward Richie with Flappy perched on one shoulder. Pernicious crouched on his other shoulder, while Nik walked alongside on the ground, holding Nat's pant leg like a child and sniffing the ground like a hunting dog. Ten feet from Richie, Nik stopped, looked up, and pointed at him.

"Thank you, Nik, Flappy," Nat said quietly.

Richie sat staring. He'd seen the little demons before in the house, but he still didn't quite believe in them. Nat pulled out the puzzle box and twisted the lid. The little demons moved near its opening, and the box sucked them in like wisps of smoke.

Nat secured the lid with a complex series of twists. "Excuse me, you're Richie, aren't you?" he said.

Richie just stared.

"Excuse me," Nat repeated.

"Huh?"

"I'm looking for a boy named Richie, and he looks exactly like you."

Richie stood up, unnerved. "What do you want?"

"I want my book back." Nat tossed Richie's backpack at his feet. He motioned for Richie to hand over the *DK Journal*. Richie hesitated.

Nat pointed. "If you don't hand over my book right now . . . ," he warned. The snake staff writhed in his hand.

"Whoa!" Richie almost fell over himself. He shoved the *Journal* at Nat. Nat grabbed it and clutched it to his chest.

Richie stood by, wondering if he should run, but Nat didn't do anything except hug his book. He didn't look mad, just relieved. Richie grew curious. "How did you find me?" he asked.

"By abandoning logic and immersing myself in the chaos of the streets," Nat said.

"Huh?"

Nat rolled his eyes. "I picked up your trail from the guy playing the spoons back there in Pioneer Square. He said some kid had just walked by talking crazy about monsters."

"I ain't crazy, man. Some street people are, but I ain't."

"I believe you." Nat nodded. "I know that the Beast you released is quite real."

Something told Richie that, despite the snake staff in his hand and the little monsters in the box, this kid wasn't the problem. "My friend Gus," Richie said, "he's . . . gone, isn't he?"

Nat frowned but didn't answer. Instead, he turned to go, motioning for Richie to follow. "Come with me."

"I don't know, man. . . ." Richie hesitated.

Nat cast him a backward glance. "The Beast tracks its prey."

Moments later Nat strode from the alley with Richie hustling after him, checking over his shoulder.

• • •

Nat walked quickly toward Pike Place Market. He tucked the demon box back into his pocket.

Richie bounced after Nat, pointing at the box. "Dude, what is that?"

"What is what?"

"The three little mutant things and that box sucking them up. And they're all going *whoosh*, right inside, like it's a monster vacuum or something."

Nat stopped, brow furrowed. "You saw that?"

"No," Richie snapped, "I just like making weird stuff up."

Nat stomped his foot. "I mean it, did you receive a clear visual image of three demonic manifestations that are minionic in character?"

"I saw a pint-sized dragon, a deformed evil gnome on steroids, and a retarded, two-legged Chihuahua."

"So you *did* see them," Nat said.

Richie looked Nat straight in the eye. "Yeah. So what gives?"

Nat looked around to see if anyone was watching.

He grabbed Richie by the shirt and pulled him nose to nose. He stared into Richie's eyes as though trying to look into his very soul.

Richie squirmed. "Dude, you are *way* inside my comfort zone."

"They are my minions," Nat said. "But I can't believe you saw them out here in the wild." Nat looked him up and down, holding him like a dog by the collar and practically sniffing him. "This is incredible."

"Okay, man, who are you?" Richie tried to sound tough. "I mean, I've seen some weird things in my life, but the stuff I've seen in the last twenty-four hours is totally freakin' me out."

Nat spoke in a distant, ominous voice. "If I tell you, the world will never look the same to you again." He pulled Richie's eyelid up to look into Richie's eye like an amateur optometrist. "Do you really want to know?"

"Jeez, I dunno. Now you're actin' all creepy and stuff."

Nat loosened his grip on Richie's collar, deepened his voice, and raised his arms. "Listen to me. And I tell you this only because of what you can see. I am Nathaniel Grimlock! I see things others cannot, and I am trained to tame pure chaos."

Nat let the words sink in, then grabbed Richie's shoulder and started him moving again. "Humans seek order. The creatures you've seen live to disrupt. And in the middle there is me, a supernatural referee. For I am, you see, a Keeper of demons."

Nat let go, satisfied that he'd made an impression. "Any questions?"

Richie stared at the ground, thinking. Finally, he looked up at Nat.

"You're a Demonkeeper?"

Nat nodded. "I am."

"You keep track of those *things*?"

"I do."

"So last night when my friend was getting eaten by one . . ."

Nat frowned.

". . . where were you?"

Nat looked at his shoes. The deep authority in his voice vanished. "Let's keep moving."

CHAPTER 33

Hunting Strays

The Beast glided through the alley. It crept from the shadows to sniff a steaming grate. The smell of the human boy wafted up from the metal. The scent was still fresh. The Beast tracked quickly along the pavement, heading toward Pike Place Market.

The Beast emerged from the alley and glanced about, yellow eyes searching the crowd for its prey. It did not have to worry about being seen. Despite its bulk and the menacing tools of dismemberment that filled its mouth, most humans looked right past it, unable to see it or refusing to. A few special humans could see it or sense it was there, but those humans could usually be avoided, or eaten if necessary.

A vendor nearby chased a cat from his stall, shaking his fist. "Darned strays!" The cat scuttled off into an alley.

The Beast lifted its head from the ground. Drops of drool dribbled out between its sharp teeth. It was close to catching the boy, but the stray kitty was within sight, tantalizing. It had been hours since it had eaten. It could pick up the boy's scent again after it had a little snack. The Beast licked its black lips and bounded off into the alley after the cat.

CHAPTER 34

Pike Place Market

Nat strode through the market with Richie right behind him.

"Where are we going?" asked Richie.

"You'll know when I get there," Nat said.

"Why are we in such a hurry now anyway? There's people around. I don't think . . ."

Nat spun, walking backward. "No," he snapped, "you don't!" He scowled. "The Beast could slip past these sightless bystanders so fast your head would spin, then come off."

"How come you can see it, then?"

"I told you. I see things others cannot."

Unsatisfied, Richie mimicked him. "'I see things udders cannot, I see things udders cannot. . . .' That's not an answer."

"Look, I first saw them when I was in sixth grade, after my parents disappeared. Nobody believed me either, all right? Then a strange East Indian man showed up. He believed me. He gave me a home. He saved me. Since then, I've been trained to see all kinds of demons."

"I saw some in your house too."

"Anyone can see them in the house. They roam free there. That's no test of your ability."

"It's not that complicated," Richie argued. "You just look, and there they are, like your mini-ones I saw in the alley just now."

" 'Minions.' " Nat bristled. "Listen, maybe you have some ability, but if your sight has just begun to develop, you don't simply 'look, and there they are.' " It had taken Nat a lot of training to see demons clearly outside the house. He wasn't about to believe that Richie could see them so easily.

They rounded a corner, stepping into the market. Florists, fruit sellers, and fishmongers filled the square. They were packing up their tables for the evening and attending to their last few customers.

Nat stopped. He gestured with a sweeping arm. "You want a real test? Try telling me if there are any in this square."

Richie squinted. "I'm lookin'. . . ."

"You can't 'look' for them. The harder you look, the more the world appears the way you expect. The human mind distorts what's really there into what you think should be there, what your logic will accept. You have to relax your brain. If you can learn *not* to look, perhaps someday you will *see*."

Nat glanced at the life-size bronze pig sculpture in the middle of the market. Richie followed his eyes, frowning doubtfully. He took a deep breath and stared. For a moment nothing happened. Then the pig's metal tail twitched slightly.

Richie squinted. Wrong move. The pig went still.

Nat began to walk away. "Let's go."

Richie ignored him and tried to relax again, doing an exaggerated tai chi movement he'd seen in a martial arts movie. It worked; he did relax. And slowly, the pig rotated its metal head and winked at him.

Richie's jaw dropped. He breathed slowly and continued to relax. He let his eyes float without directing or focusing them anywhere in particular. Gradually, as though emerging from a giant 3-D hidden picture, the market's other demons eased into focus.

A glistening green slime demon slid between fruit at a vendor's table. When a woman reached down for an apple, it oozed over her hand, causing her to scream and upset the apple cart. She yanked her hand away and looked but caught only a fleeting glimpse of the goo before the vendor's pyramid of apples toppled. The slime dripped through a crack and slithered away, leaving the vendor and the woman barking at each other about bruised apples and green vomit that was no longer there.

Across the street, a flame demon leapt from candle to candle so that each time the candle vendor turned around, a different candle was lit. She looked puzzled and concerned, but she couldn't quite figure out what was wrong.

Nearby, a thin crack in the sidewalk moved underfoot to trip a small boy with an ice cream cone. The boy went down, and the ice cream flew. As the boy gathered himself, his mother barked, "Be more careful!" The boy began to cry and pointed to where he had tripped, but by then the crack had moved away.

Richie watched it all with wide eyes. He couldn't help grabbing Nat's sleeve and pointing excitedly. "Oh yeah! There! And there! And over there! No way!"

Nat saw them too. He stared, amazed, at Richie. "You really do see them, don't you?"

"Yeah! Over there and there and . . ."

Suddenly, Richie ran to the pig and hopped on. "Giddyup, dude!"

Nat chased Richie. "No!" Nat hit him in the midsection with a flying tackle, knocking him off the disgruntled pig. They went to the ground hard and lay there together. Nat whispered to Richie through clenched teeth, "Do not taunt the pig."

They rose, dirty and sore. Nat dusted Richie off as though tending to a younger brother, while people stared. He spoke loudly enough for the gawkers to hear. "How many times has Dad told you not to ride statues?!" Nat hustled Richie away from the puzzled crowd, speaking in a harsh whisper again. "They're hiding from humans. Don't draw them out. They create havoc when they're aroused. Besides, there's too many of them here. Something's wrong."

Nearby, the fishmongers shouted and hurled fish to one another through the crowd. One flying salmon turned its head toward Nat as it flew by. "Run!" it whispered.

Nat grabbed Richie's arm and did as the salmon advised.

• • •

The sloping head and hulking shoulders of the Beast surfaced from the pavement behind a Dumpster in the alley. The Beast scanned the crowd. The end of a furry little calico tail dangled from its mouth. It realized the tail was protruding and slurped it in like a wayward strand of spaghetti.

Then it saw the boys hurrying away from the fishmonger's booth. It grinned and melted back into the asphalt, following its prey like an ocean swell in the pavement.

CHAPTER 35

Nat Has Some
Explaining to Do

Nat and Richie hurried along the elevated Alaskan Way Viaduct that ran beside the Seattle waterfront. With the sun dipping behind the Olympic Mountains across the bay, the docks below were closed down and empty. The missing crowds gave the area a haunted feel. It was odd that so few people were about. But Richie didn't seem bothered. He bounced along, humming, as though a horrible creature with fangs and claws wasn't a part of his world. The kid either had powerful nerves, thought Nat, or a short-term memory disorder.

"So what are demons anyway?" Richie asked suddenly.

"Not a good time to chat."

"I think I have a right to know, seeing as one's trying to eat me and all," he said.

Not a bad point, Nat admitted to himself. "Invisible random energy surrounds us," he explained, "like drifts of fog. When random energy gathers, it becomes chaos. When chaos gathers, it can form a demon. Get it?"

Richie shook his head. "No."

Nat tried again. "Demons are bundles of chaotic energy that consolidate into a visual image, or a sound, or even a physical shape. Each demon takes its form from the type of chaos that gave birth to it. For instance, rush hour fills the roads with random sound energy. An audio demon might spring to life from the concentrated auditory chaos of a traffic jam." Nat found he was twirling his hand in a little circle, the way Dhaliwahl had done when explaining something to him. He stuffed it in his pocket abruptly.

Richie stopped suddenly.

Nat frowned. "Don't stop. Why are you stopping? Stopping is something you do when a huge demon with razor-sharp claws and three-inch incisors is *not* following you."

Richie stared straight ahead. "It's not following us."

"How can you possibly know that?"

"Because it's right there," Richie said, "in front of us."

CHAPTER 36

Live Bait

Nat looked up. The Beast slowly morphed from the concrete and clung to the wall of the viaduct above them, its powerful muscles standing out even through its thick fur. Its grimacing teeth were tinted pink, as though it had recently fed, but it did not appear satiated. It scanned the waterfront hungrily, looking for them.

Nat had never seen anything more than the Beast's arm before. He stared in awe until Richie snapped him out of it with an urgent whisper. "Why don't you just suck it into the box or send it back to hell or something?"

"It's not from hell," Nat hissed back. "That's devils, not demons."

"Then how do you kill it?"

"I don't kill demons." Nat pulled Richie behind a concrete pillar, out of the Beast's sight. "I keep them."

Demonkeeper

"I don't think this is the time for a personal ethics debate," Richie said.

"Keepers do *not* kill," Nat insisted.

The Beast dropped from the upper level. It began sniffing around, trying to pick up their scent. Near the next pillar, it paused and grinned. It had found Richie's trail.

Richie grabbed Nat by the sleeve. "Now what?!"

"It's looking for you, so if we can just slip around it and lure it back to the house . . ."

Richie's eyes went wide. "Wait a minute," he gasped. "I'm bait?"

"Not . . . exactly."

Richie stared at Nat in horror. "I thought you were here to help me!"

Too loud. The Beast looked up.

Richie looked up too and realized he'd been spotted. He turned back to Nat, this time with a sad expression. "I trusted you," he said. Then he bolted, tossing down his skateboard, leaping on, and racing away.

Nat reached out after him. "Wait, Richie! I . . . I . . ." Richie disappeared down the off-ramp, and Nat mumbled his last two words to himself. ". . . I'm sorry."

Nat turned to the Beast. It was coming, like a semi truck. Nat stepped out from behind the pillar, flipping madly through the *Demonkeeper Journal*. He tried to snap the droopy snake into a firm staff, but it flopped forward, limp. He panicked. His hands shook as he tried to read a passage. " 'Heed my words,' " he read aloud, " 'for I am your Keeper.' " The Beast did not heed. In fact, it dropped to all six limbs and charged. Nat flipped back one page. "Wait . . . no, okay." He tried again. " 'Hear . . . *hear* my words.' " Nat looked up again. No luck and too late. The Beast bore down on him. Nat could see its glistening teeth and hear its eager panting. There was nothing else he could do. He turned and jumped.

The Beast swiped with a huge claw, grazing Nat as he leapt over the concrete rail. With Nat suddenly gone, it charged past, hot on Richie's trail. It didn't even look back.

Twelve feet below, Nat hit the asphalt hard. The *Journal* landed nearby. Nat groaned with his last conscious breath, rolled onto his stomach, and everything went black.

CHAPTER 37

Bad to Worse

Nat didn't know how long he'd been facedown on the pavement, only that a significant amount of time had passed before he heard the footsteps. He didn't especially want to see anyone at the moment, but he recognized that he could use some assistance. So when a thin hand reached down, as if to help him, Nat reached up to it.

But the hand didn't help him. Instead, it snatched his wrist and lifted him higher and higher, until his feet dangled six inches off the ground. He hung staring into a skeletal face.

The Thin Man held Nat aloft with a steady strength impossible for his withered limbs. His pupilless eyes were completely black and unblinking. Steam rolled from his nostrils, though it wasn't cold outside. When he spoke, he hissed as though he were a tire going flat.

"Ahhh, Dhaliwahl'sss little protégé, eh? Pleassse allow me to introduccce myself. . . ."

He flung Nat through the air. Nat landed in a crumpled heap nearby, his ears ringing. He craned his neck to see his attacker.

The Thin Man approached, leisurely and smug. Charr danced at the end of his bony finger, and Wedge preceded him as he walked, announcing him with mini-rumbles as it split the cement in two. Nat recognized them. They were the demons from the market.

"I undersssstand that Dhaliwahl isss gone." The Thin Man grinned and kicked Nat over with his foot. "But enough pleasssantriesss."

"Who are you?" Nat managed from quivering lips.

The Thin Man shook his head. "Oh, now that'sss sssad. He didn't even tell you about me, did he?" The Thin Man pointed Charr at Nat. The little demon glowed blue-hot at the end of his finger, like the flame of a welding torch. "Don't worry, ssson, it won't matter to you who I am for much longer. But there are a couple of questionsss to which I need answersss."

The Thin Man lowered Charr toward Nat's face. Nat lashed out with the snake staff. It stiffened momentarily and connected with the Thin Man's left shin.

Whack!

The Thin Man yelped in pain and limped quickly out of range.

Nat saw his chance. He struggled to crawl away, digging for the puzzle box. "Minions! Help!"

Nik, Flappy, and Pernicious tumbled out of the box.

"Three minionsss?" The Thin Man paused, taken aback by the appearance of so many minions. "Bah!" he barked finally, and he pointed his own minions toward Nik, Flappy, and Pernicious. "Dessstroy them!"

Charr leapt from his finger and raced across the ground, forming a quick circle of fire around Nik and Pernicious. Though brawny as a miniature ox, Nik cowered, terrified by the flames. But Pernicious wasn't scared. He leapt over Charr's scorching tendrils and bounced toward the Thin Man like a rubber ball. At the last moment, the Thin Man opened his mouth and vomited forth Goop. The gooey demon flew from the Thin Man's mouth and hit Pernicious broadside, dropping him to the ground in a dripping tangle.

The Thin Man laughed. "'Minionsss, help'? Isss that what the old man taught you, boy? Well, I'll let you in on a little sssecret I've learned sssince I've been on my own. You don't asssk minionsss to help, you order them to sssserve!"

The Thin Man pointed at Nat, and Wedge sliced through the pavement past him. It ran up a brick wall, which immediately began to crack and crumble. Bricks tumbled down, pounding Nat's legs as he tried to crawl out of the way. He caught a glimpse of Flappy, who was also being pelted by falling bricks.

The Thin Man approached Nat again, taking his time. Nat staggered to his feet, unsteady. The *Demonkeeper's Journal* was between him and the Thin Man. He reached out to it, but it was too late. The Thin Man was closer.

"Well, well," the Thin Man taunted, stepping to the *Journal*, "what have we here? A little light reading?" The Thin Man bent to retrieve it.

"No!" Nat cried out in vain as the Thin Man opened it and began to flip the pages.

"I'll have to brush up on my French and my Japanessse." He grinned. "And plenty of time to learn thossse lossst languagesss." He moved toward Nat with an awful, evil smile. "But firssst thingsss firssst. Are you prepared to die, *mon ami? Tomodachi?*"

Nat looked up into the Thin Man's black eyes. "My God, you're a . . ."

". . . Keeper." The Thin Man nodded. "Like you, only ssstronger." He stepped on Nat's foot and pushed his chest like a school yard bully. Nat fell on his back. His head whipped against the pavement with a dull *thud*.

The Thin Man stood over him, looking off into the distance and talking as though thinking aloud. "We have great power, my lesss-learned colleague. For eonsss we have tended them like nanniesss, when we could easssily have ensssslaved them. I will change all of that, you sssee. The mossst clossssely guarded one of them all, the Be-assst . . . it'sss loosssse, isssn't it? Dhaliwahl wouldn't talk about it, but I know it isss sssstrong. I will add it to my army. Imagine, a creature like that at my command!"

"We don't command them," mumbled Nat from where he lay on the ground, "we keep them."

The Thin Man turned when Nat spoke, as though just remembering Nat was there. "That isss the old way," he hissed. He pulled a wavy-bladed ceremonial dagger from his trench coat and tested the edge for sharpness over Nat. "With me, thingsss will be different." He turned the knife in his hand, examining it. "Shame to be mortal, eh? But I'm working on that one too, for myssself."

Nat still couldn't catch his breath. His ankle throbbed where a brick had landed on it, and his head swam from its impact on the pavement. But with death standing over him, he found himself desperately focused. He concentrated hard, and the snake staff slowly writhed to life at his feet.

Just as the Thin Man raised the knife to finish the job, the serpent reared its head and spread its cobra hood.

The Thin Man stopped in his tracks, no longer smiling or joking, but deadly serious. "You can't posssibly know how to ussse that," he growled. But Nat could hear uncertainty in his voice.

Nat huddled behind the guardian snake, his own voice shaking. "Come on ahead and see." Nik, Flappy, and Pernicious limped back to him, as burned, beaten, and weak as he was. Nat gathered them into the box.

The snake wove back and forth, and the Thin Man kept his distance. "Eh, I need not worry about you." He sounded annoyed. "You are weak. You'll never have the will to defy me." He spat on the ground to show his disgust. "You are fading even now." He tucked the *DK Journal* in his trench coat, and his own minions flocked to him.

Shivering, exhausted, and dizzy, Nat struggled to keep from blacking out as it began to rain. Fainting in the gutter would mean death. Though Nat wasn't sure that would be the worst thing in the world.

The Thin Man stood just beyond the reach of the snake's fangs, waiting for Nat's concentration to fail. It did. Nat blinked and swayed. The snake faltered, stiffened into the staff, and clattered to the pavement. The Thin Man gripped the knife and stepped forward.

But just before Nat collapsed on the ground, two bright lights illuminated his misery. A car stuttered to a stop beside him. The passenger door opened, and the shadowy driver peered out into the downpour. Nat stared up. Like a good dream after a nightmare, Sandy's face smiled down at him.

"You know, I'm torn," she said. "Am I lucky I found you or an idiot for looking?"

With the last of his strength, Nat grabbed the door and hauled himself up into the passenger seat.

"Drive!" Nat groaned.

Sandy frowned. "Now wait a minute . . ."

Suddenly, green goop splattered across her windshield. A small flame leapt up onto her hood. The Thin Man's bony face appeared at her driver's side window. Sandy yelped.

"Drive!" Nat barked again. He slammed his foot down on Sandy's atop the gas pedal, and the Volvo lurched forward.

Charr was thrown clear. Nat flipped on the windshield wipers. The wiper blade hit Goop and swept the slimy little demon over the side of the car onto the wet pavement, where the rear tire squashed him into a paperthin layer of ooze. As the Volvo moved, the Thin Man disappeared into the rearview mirror.

Behind the car, the street erupted, cracking down the middle. The fissure in the ground followed the car, tearing the asphalt asunder.

"Go! Go!" Nat yelled.

"What's going on?" Sandy said, shrugging off Nat's foot.

"It's right behind us!"

Sandy had trouble shifting. She hit the gas, but the Volvo only sputtered.

Wedge tore toward the stalled car, opening a trench in the street. Sandy ground the gears once, twice, then finally yanked the shifter into place. They screeched forward just as Wedge arrived. Sandy turned a corner, bounced off the curb, and sped down the road. Nat looked back. The street behind them was a gaping hole large enough to bury the car, but they were outdistancing it. "Faster! Straighter! Watch out! Go!" he yelled.

"I just got my license!" Sandy yelled back, but she kept her foot on the pedal, and they flew by the docks, up the hill, and into downtown.

CHAPTER 38

Out of the Frying Pan

Richie walked down a steep Seattle street, skateboard stuffed in his backpack, his shoes splashing through the shallow river the heavy rain had created atop the asphalt. The abject terror had worn off a few blocks back. Now he just felt nervous and jumpy. He didn't know where to go but knew he should keep moving.

Richie pulled the hood of his sweatshirt over his head against the rain, even though the cloth was already soaked. Beside him, a fish wriggled along the pavement, moving uphill past him. He stared. It was a salmon. He grinned, amused. "What the . . . fish?" He chuckled.

He spotted another salmon nearby, then another. He stopped and watched. Soon the entire street was filled with salmon migrating up the hill. They swam by him, leaping and floundering upstream against the rain runoff.

Richie cocked his head. Had they come through a drainpipe from the ocean? The frantic scene was almost funny, except that the salmon looked sort of desperate. Richie watched them tumble over one another. They were stampeding away from something.

Richie stopped grinning and backed away uphill, unnerved. Whatever the salmon were running from, it was down below, at the bottom of the hill in the darkest shadows. He squinted into the night, then he remembered what Nat had said about seeing demons—if you did *not* look hard enough, you could see them. So he tried not to look but instead just to see. And he did.

There was a strange lump in the street at the bottom of the hill. It moved uphill toward him, burrowing through the sheet of water on the road like a submarine. Salmon leapt ahead of it, fleeing.

Richie began to back away but slipped and fell on his rump. He crawled backward as he saw the pavement stretch up, growing into a dark, bulky, shambling form. Moments later the Beast rose completely from the water. It pulled its legs free of the pavement and shifted to a shambling gait, splashing toward him.

Richie reached back and yanked his skateboard from his pack, raising it like a club. The Beast arrived in a spray of water and fur and grabbed for Richie. A yellow claw caught his backpack. Richie wriggled out of his pack, leapt in the air, and, at the last possible moment, shoved his board under his feet.

The Beast looked up, pieces of shredded backpack hanging from its mouth. It saw Richie bombing down the hill, a rooster tail of water fanning out behind his board's spinning wheels.

And the chase was on.

Richie rode the steep hill, propelled at rocket speed by gravity. He navigated parked cars, mailboxes, and parking meters, bending his body at impossible angles to turn his board. The Beast splashed after him, scrambling over cars, leaping fire hydrants, and knocking a parking meter flat.

A car turned onto the street. Richie swerved and grabbed the bumper, hitching a ride. The Beast galloped after him, then stopped in the middle of the street and sniffed, sensing something. A bus . . .

Wham! The bus struck the Beast dead center with its grill. *Thump-bump! Thump-bump!*

Richie looked back. The bus driver looked puzzled, wondering what she'd hit. Richie gripped the car's bumper tight, turned his attention to staying atop his board, and tucked to make sure he didn't wipe out.

Blocks later, Richie let go of the car and glided into

an alley. He'd gotten away. His blood was still pumping from the chase, but the feeling wasn't good like a thrill-seeking high. He gasped for breath and shook from the cold and rain. He had to get some sleep, or soon he wouldn't be able to tell which hallucinations were hallucinations and which were real demons. A mistake could be fatal.

As he drifted along on his board, thinking and losing momentum, a crack appeared just ahead of him in the sidewalk. His skateboard hit the fissure and pitched him head over heels onto his back with a heavy "ummph!" Richie swore, groaning. When he looked up, a yelp froze in his throat. He found himself staring right into a pair of eyes. But they weren't the beady yellow eyes of the Beast. They were the all-black eyes of the Thin Man.

CHAPTER 39

Heading Home

Sandy drove. Despite her inexperience, she'd managed to navigate Seattle's downtown. She'd also destroyed a hubcap on a curb, forced a bicycle cop into a shrub, and obliterated a mailbox.

The interior of Sandy's car was neat as a pin, except for her passenger, who was a dripping mess. Sandy looked over, frowning. Nat shook as he tried to stuff a strange box into his pocket.

"W-w-where are we g-going?" He shivered.

"Someplace dry."

"But I need to stay on the street, keep looking."

"You need a towel, some hot tea, maybe some psychotropic medication."

Nat didn't seem to have the energy to argue. He sat silent as they eased through the rain.

"I had him," he mumbled finally, half to himself.

"Richie?"

"But then he disappeared, poof, as if he was a phantom." Nat slumped in his seat. "Although I'm sure he's not."

Sandy wrinkled her brow. "Did you get your book back?"

"Yeah . . . ," he muttered. Nat faded. His head lolled on his shoulder. ". . . but it disappeared again too."

Nat's eyes were closed. Sandy wasn't getting answers. "Richie's not going to stay out in this weather," she said. "He'll hide somewhere. Give it up tonight, huh?"

Her words fell on deaf ears. Nat had passed out.

• • •

The Thin Man strode through the sleepy Queen Anne Hill neighborhood, a light mist all about him and a bulging, Richie-size canvas bag trailing behind with tennis shoes sticking out. He pulled it along the ground like a bloodhound lure, making sure to leave twin tennis shoe trails on the damp sidewalk for the Beast to follow. The *DK Journal* was tucked under his arm.

CHAPTER 40
Sandy's Place

Nat stirred and found a pillow under his head. There was also a clock beside him. It was three in the morning. He snapped awake, threw off the pillow, and cursed himself for having fallen asleep. He sat up and looked around.

He sat in a tidy basement room. In the dimness he could make out a little couch with a quilt neatly folded over one arm. A small desk sat in the corner with school-books stacked symmetrically atop it and its chair pushed in. A shelf nearby was lined with paperback books arranged smallest to tallest. The room looked unlived in, like a room in a catalog.

Sandy's room, he thought.

Nat swung his legs over the edge of the bed and discovered that he was dressed in pink flannel pajamas. His wet clothes hung drying on a hook next to the bed. He didn't remember changing clothes. Nat squinted in the darkness. He could make out a dark lump on the little couch. Sandy.

Nat slid off the bed and quickly replaced the pajamas with his own damp, clammy clothes. He crossed the room to where Sandy slept on the couch and crouched beside her sleeping form. She looked peaceful lying there, angelic against the fluffy white pillow. He didn't want to disturb her, but the demonic world wouldn't wait, and he had already wasted too much time.

"Sandra . . . ," he whispered. "Sandy."

Sandy rolled over. It was her turn to be half asleep. "Huh? What?"

"I have to go."

Sandy leaned out to look at the clock. "What time is it?"

"Time for me to go."

"Nat, you've had a rough night. You were practically unconscious when I found you. Go back to sleep. Besides, my parents might hear us. It will be safer to sneak you out of here in the morning."

"That's too late!"

Sandy groaned and rose. "Nat, this is ridiculous. You're asking me to sneak my parents' car and leave in the middle of the night. The police probably have my license plate number. Why do you have to go now?"

"It's tough to explain."

"You make no sense," Sandy said, pulling on her socks.

"What do you mean?" said Nat.

"I mean this whole evening's been totally weird."

"Weird?"

Sandy nodded, exasperated. "Yes, Nat, weird. It was weird to chase a street kid around the city, it was weird to find you waterlogged in the gutter and have some creepy man throw green goo on my parents' car, it's weird for me to run from the police, it's totally weird to have a boy in my room with me alone, and it's weird to have that same boy slinking off at the deepest, darkest hour of the night."

She took a deep breath. "You're just . . ." Sandy waved her hand in circles, thinking.

Nat looked at his shoes and finished her sentence for her. ". . . a weirdo."

Sandy immediately felt horrible. She wanted to take it all back. But she couldn't think of anything to say that wouldn't just make it worse. Instead, she said nothing and pushed past Nat into the bathroom.

Nat sat on the couch, awaiting her return. There was

a stir in his pocket. He didn't have the will to stop them. His minions climbed out of the box onto the couch. Nat looked at his battered snake staff on the floor, then at Flappy, whose injured wing hung limp. Nik's face was still singed and blackened. Pernicious had his finger stuffed far up his nose.

"Look at us," Nat said. "We're pathetic. Me most of all." He stood and motioned them back in the box. "Come on, we're going home."

CHAPTER 41

More Trouble at Home

The typically boisterous foyer of Nat's home went quiet as the last lock on the front door fell away. The dead-bolt mechanism and a circle of wood around it dropped into the entryway as though carved out by a blowtorch from the outside. There was a hollow *boom*, and the door flew open. The Thin Man stepped across the threshold with Charr burning at the end of his finger. Richie's head and feet protruded from the large bag he dragged behind him. He dropped Richie to the wood floor with a heavy thump and surveyed the house, his sour, skeletal expression turning to an unpleasant grin.

Richie lay on the floor, wrapped in the Thin Man's bag like an oversized burrito. He craned his neck, wondering where his captor had gone.

"Uh, dude?" He looked about, recognizing for the

first time that he was in the old house where all the trouble had begun. He squirmed. "Dude . . . ?"

Suddenly, the Thin Man loomed over him, nose to nose and looking at him upside down. "Yesss."

Richie's first instinct was to shut his eyes. But after having been dragged through the streets of Seattle for an hour, he knew that the face wouldn't go away. He cocked an eyebrow. "So, what's your deal, man?"

The Thin Man leaned in, his foggy breath flowing over Richie. His hissing voice leaked between his bony teeth. "There'sss sssomething incredible out there, and it ssseemsss to be following you. But you already know that, don't you?" He paused, but not long enough for Richie to answer. "When it arrivesss, I shall feed it. I shall make it my sssoldier."

Feed it what? Richie wondered.

The Thin Man surveyed the foyer, talking to himself. "Decadesss ago I walked thessse hallsss. I have quessstionsss . . . yesss, many quessstionsss. You are obviousssly the apprentisss's apprentisss. Tell me, apprentisss, what sssort of colosssal ssstupidity allowed the Beasssst to essscape?"

Richie bit his lip. The Thin Man approached the basement door. The flickering wooden lamp nearby leaned away as the Thin Man passed. He bent over to examine

Demonkeeper

the door. "I could ussse a little light on the back door here," he said to the wooden lamp.

The little lamp twisted slightly and trained its circle of light directly on the Thin Man's skinny rump.

The Thin Man glanced behind himself, and his eyebrows arched. "A comedian, eh?" He stood up straight, lip curling back in a sneer. "It'sss time I ssset an example."

He snapped his fingers, and Charr appeared at his fingertip again. He raised his arms and his slithery words wound through the house. "Creaturesss of chaosss, hear my name! I, Ian Fortusss, am your massster now, and when I sssnap my fingersss, you will do as I sssay. And make no mistake, if you do not obey, I'll sssend you back to the abysss whenccce you came!"

With a crooked smirk, he swung his burning finger across the wooden lamp. The shade caught fire, and the lamp wailed. Charr spread quickly. The burning wooden base began to writhe in pain. It leapt to the floor, yanking its own cord from the wall. The lamp danced an obscene, anguished jig as Charr ate it alive.

Across the room, the clock's hands whirled madly, the Indian rug shifted nervously, and the carved heads atop the bench stared in mute horror.

Soon, thankfully, the lamp's screams faded away. Its cloth shade was in cinders, and its wooden base was a blackened corpse. The shade's circular metal frame clattered to the floor. A bare bulb fell out and rolled in a slow circle.

The lamp was dead.

Charr returned to the Thin Man's finger. "Lightsssout," he hissed. He raised his voice again so that all of the demons in the home could hear him. "Isss anyone elssse confusssed about who isss in charge?!" The Thin Man waved his hand. A broom scooted out of the hall closet and began sweeping up obediently. The Thin Man folded his arms and smiled. "They will ssserve me," he whispered to himself. "Dhaliwahl wasss wrong. . . ."

He surveyed the room. No demon could have missed the screams of the dying lamp. He knew they were listening. He smiled. "I'm going to the ssstudy," he announced. "While I'm there, sssomeone find the dog . . . and kill it."

CHAPTER 42
Relentless

The Beast held Richie's skateboard in its claws. It sniffed the wood and wheels for a moment, discarded the board, and began sniffing along the ground again. The board smelled of young boy, stray young boy. The Beast sensed it was on the right trail, a trail that led out of downtown Seattle and back in the direction of the house it knew so well.

The Beast hesitated, its primitive brain remembering captivity. But hunger was stronger. The taste of stray boy lingered on the strange board its prey had left behind.

Beyond the board, the scent path suddenly grew stronger, as though the boy had begun dragging some part of his body full on the ground instead of rolling on wheels above it. The track was clear now. The Beast grinned, all memory of imprisonment forgotten. With an eager grunt, it romped off in the direction of the boy's scent.

CHAPTER 43

100 Percent Failure

Sandy pulled up to the curb and began her parallel-park routine. Nat was too polite to complain and too weary to suggest that a crooked parking job was sufficient for dumping off an unwanted weirdo. He simply slouched and waited until she was done.

Finally, they were parked. He looked up. She did too. To Nat's horror, they were looking directly at each other again.

"Nathaniel," Sandy said, as though just staring at each other at close range wasn't bad enough, "I just wanted to say that, no matter what, it's nice what you did for Richie."

"I don't understand."

"I mean not calling the authorities on him. Trying to handle it yourself."

Nat shook his head. "I don't think I did him any good."

"But you tried. With a lost kid like that, if you at least tried, you already did some good."

Nat opened his door and climbed out. "I have to, um, sort out some things. Unless you want more weirdness in your life, I think I'd better do it alone." He pushed the door closed. It made a loud *whump* that sounded as hollow as his heart felt.

Nat walked up the path and mounted the front steps, but when he set his foot on the porch, it writhed and threw him off into the grass.

"Hey!" he complained, getting up to his hands and knees and brushing dirt from his pants. "Knock it off."

He rose and tried again, holding on to the rail and placing his foot gingerly near the center of the porch. Same reaction. The deck heaved, pushing his leg first one direction, then another. This time Nat was ready. He pulled himself hand over hand along the rail and struggled to the door, balancing on the undulating porch.

He saw the holes burned through the door where the locks used to be. He reached for the doorknob, puzzled and concerned. It moved. He reached again. It dodged away from his hand. "What are you doing?" he said. Suddenly, the porch bucked. It rose in a huge wave, carried him to its edge, and dumped him off onto the sparse grass again.

• • •

As Sandy pulled away, she took one last sad look in the rearview mirror. She expected to see Nat shuffle up his steps and out of her life forever. Instead, she saw Nat fly off the porch, through the air, and onto the grass. He sprawled there for a moment, rubbing his head.

Sandy's eyes narrowed. It was true—Nat was weird. But the words *weird* and *intriguing* weren't so different. He had stood up for her at the mall, and there was no denying that he needed her help.

"U go girl," she reminded herself. She parked the car at a crazy angle with one tire up on the curb, killed the engine, jumped out, and started back toward Nat's house.

• • •

Nat stood on the lawn rubbing his head, perplexed. He picked up the puzzle box, which had fallen from his pocket. Flappy was already free, and Pernicious's head was hanging out, looking around. Nat shook Pernicious and Nik out onto the ground. Something was not right, he thought, more not right than usual.

Nat walked around the side of the house, avoiding the porch and singed door. The little demons hopped after him, as curious about what he was up to as they were pleased to be freed from the little box again. Nat walked past the study window. He glanced inside, then pressed his face to the glass. What he saw brought the final curtain of despair down on his nightmare day.

"Oh no . . ."

Inside, the Thin Man was removing the sacred urns from the shelf. Dhaliwahl's urn was first. He tumbled it into a bag. *Clunk!* He moved down the row, pulling down each Keeper's urn from its place of honor. Next into the bag was Yatabe the Wanderer. *Clunk!* Then LeFevre, then McFeen. *Clunk! Clunk!*

Another lumpy bag sat on a nearby table, while a terrified study lamp swung back and forth to provide light for the Thin Man as he directed demons about like a drill sergeant. Every mobile demon in Nat's house was lined up before the Thin Man in regimented rows—a strutting coffee table, living dust bunnies, the walking bookshelf, and many more. It was a small army. Even the demons that Nat himself could never control were obeying the Thin Man.

Nat slumped and slid down the outside of the house, defeated. After all of Dhaliwahl's trust and careful teaching, he'd been a disaster.

Seeing Nat slumped there, Flappy straightened his injured wing and hopped over to him. Nik flexed his huge, tiny muscles. Pernicious puffed his skinny chest.

Nat looked up and shook his head. "What do you want me to do? We got our tails kicked last time, and that was before I lost the *Journal* to him. I lost the Beast too. And now I've lost the entire house. As a Keeper, I'm a complete, total, one hundred percent failure."

The minions stared at Nat, somber as three stone gargoyles. Nat looked away down the hill. In the distance, a dark, hunched shadow loped toward the house with its nose to the ground. It was the Beast. He stiffened.

But instead of terror this time, Nat felt a twinge, a Keeper's instinct perhaps. Even with death lumbering toward him, he felt the need to look in the window one more time instead of flee. He moved to get a better angle on the second lumpy bag he had seen on the study table. When he looked closer, he saw the bag move. There was someone in it.

"Richie . . . ," he gasped.

CHAPTER 44

Breaking Back In

Nat hung from the snake staff fifteen feet off the ground. The snake wound itself around the rain gutter over his second-floor bedroom window. Nik and Pernicious clung to the side of the house like rock outcroppings with one of Nat's feet on each of their backs. Flappy, who enjoyed the luxury of flight, sat atop the window.

Nat pulled himself up with great effort. He had to help Richie. He could give up as a Keeper, but he couldn't leave the kid that had trusted him behind to be devoured. Nat reached for his window while Pernicious scurried up onto his head like a limber squirrel. The little demon shape-shifted into two dimensions and slid through a crack in the casing.

Once inside, Pernicious popped back into three dimensions. Nat pointed him to the latch, which Pernicious puzzled over for an excruciatingly long time. Looking down, Nat contemplated which of his bones were most likely to break if Pernicious didn't hurry.

After what seemed an eternity, Pernicious unlocked the window. Nat summoned all his strength, held on with one hand, and pushed the window up with the other. The window hitched upward with a loud squeak. Nat cringed as the snake staff struggled to hold him up. He gritted his teeth against his burning muscles and pushed on the window again. This time the window gave more easily, with only a slight whine. Nat heaved himself up.

He tumbled into his bedroom. The snake staff hung limp, spent from the climb. When Nik and Flappy were inside too, Nat looked around. His bed was stripped. There was something large wrapped in his comforter in the corner of the room. It made noise, a muffled whimpering. Nat started toward it.

Suddenly, the comforter exploded from the thing in the corner and flew at Nat. It wrapped around his head. Nat stumbled, pulling at it and fighting to breathe. Nik, Flappy, and Pernicious dove in. Each seized a corner. They pulled in separate directions. The comforter unfolded, and Nat rolled out like a peeled banana, gasping for breath.

Nat motioned, and they brought their corners together, struggling to control the mad bedding. Nat grabbed the fourth corner. They folded the bedding again and again until it was a harmless square. Nat held it on the floor, and his three minions, mostly Nik, heaved a dresser atop it, where it struggled, trapped.

Nat turned to the corner of the room. Lying there, barely breathing, was Bel. Nat hurried to him. The great dog was on its side, motionless. Nat knew that the bedding didn't have the malice to smother Bel on its own. Nat patted Bel. The huge dog would have to sit tight.

"All right," he said to his minions, "he may have turned the rest of the house against us too, so keep your eyes peeled." With that, Nat headed for the hall. Pernicious scuttled in front of him, his bulbous eyes extending from their sockets on flexible stalks and bending to check around corners.

Nat crept down the stairs into the hallway on the main floor. So far, so good. It seemed that most of the demons were gathered in the study, leaving the rest of the house mercifully quiet. He turned to whisper to Nik and Pernicious, who were imitating his slinking walk.

"Okay, now real quiet, because—"

"Halt! Who goes there?" a voice barked.

"Intruder!" another shouted.

Nat looked up. It was the masks. "Shut up, you idiots," he hissed, "it's me."

"Me who?" snapped the wooden mask.

"Yeah, you who?" said the iron mask.

Nat didn't have time to argue with them. He grabbed the masks from their nails and chucked them to Pernicious and Nik, who clamped little claws over their mouths and hauled them off to the bedroom.

Nat pushed on, while Flappy fluttered down the hall beside him. They slipped into the foyer. Nat saw the large chunks of scorched wooden lamp that hadn't been swept up. He gasped and hurried over, but there was nothing he could do. "Careful, minions," Nat said as Nik and Pernicious rejoined them, "the house is in full chaos."

"As it should be!" The Thin Man filled the archway across the foyer. "You and your little 'moronsss' are about as ssstealthy as a herd of wild audiomorphsss." He sneered. "I do not underssstand how you can have three minionsss when you are ssso weak, but it doesn't matter." The Thin Man waved his own minions into the foyer. "Dessstroy them or be dessstroyed by me!"

Charr and Goop charged across the foyer. Wedge tore through the wood planks in the floor, splitting them as it passed.

Nat stood his ground. He held the snake staff high in one hand, concentrating, and waved his free hand.

Flappy hopped forward and struggled into a wobbly

flight. Getting airborne was a brief struggle, but swooping down was an entirely different thing. Falling was something Flappy did well.

Charr rose up in a wall of flame to block Flappy's headlong dive. But Flappy swept through the flames, blowing them aside like flimsy curtains. He plummeted downward, directly at Goop. Goop was slow, surprised, and unable to dodge. Flappy pulled up at the last second and snatched the putrid demon in his talons.

As Flappy fluttered away, Goop hung helpless from his claws, drippy but in one piece.

Wedge shot toward Nat, burrowing through an old floorboard. Nikolai stomped out from between Nat's parted legs and intercepted the charging creature. He grabbed the flooring that the vicious crack inhabited and ripped the entire board up. Holding it aloft, he gave Wedge nowhere to go.

Meanwhile, Flappy swooped in low, zeroing in on the fan. As he approached, he pulled up, dragging the glutinous, pulsating body of Goop through the whirling blades. *Splat!* Green goo spattered the wall.

The Thin Man reeled, a part of him suddenly destroyed. He threw his hand against the wall to keep from falling and roared at Charr. "Burn their Keeper!"

As the other minions engaged, Charr encircled Nat,

who stood motionless, still concentrating. Charr gathered its strength, growing higher and higher into a burning ring of fire.

Suddenly, Pernicious hopped through the wall of flame onto Nat's shoulder. He held the spray bottle that Nat used during chores to water the dead-alive plant down the hall. *Squirt!* A mist of water rained down on Charr. The dancing flame faltered and fizzled loudly, in obvious pain. Pernicious aimed again. *Squirt-squirt . . . fizzle!* Charr turned and fled across the foyer. Pernicious leapt after it, squirting and cackling madly.

"Yee-hee-hee-heeee!"

Nik thumped away down the hall to dispose of the floorboard with Wedge trapped inside.

"Imbecccilesss!" hissed the Thin Man. He pulled out his ceremonial knife and advanced on Nat himself.

Nat lowered the snake staff. Its hissing head writhed to life, holding the Thin Man at bay. Nat and the Thin Man began to stalk each other carefully as Pernicious bounced among them, chasing Charr around the room with the spray bottle like a delighted child chasing a moth.

"You don't know what it doesss, do you?" the Thin Man said, gesturing at the snake staff with his knife.

"I know you fear it," Nat replied. "That is enough."

"You amussse me, Junior Keeper. But the fact isss that you only became the lassst-minute replacccement after Dhaliwahl and I had sssome creative differencesss."

"You were Dhaliwahl's first pupil?" Nat gasped.

"For a time. I outgrew him."

"You ran away."

"I *walked* away. I had learned enough from the old man."

Nat and the Thin Man circled each other slowly until Nat found himself near the hallway that led to the study.

"Enough foolishnesss!" the Thin Man hissed. "I can kill you without my minionsss." He cocked the knife to his ear.

Nat didn't argue. Instead, he turned and ran to the study.

Demonkeeper

CHAPTER 45

The Rescue Attempt

Richie looked up as Nat burst in. "Oh, great, the other person who thinks of me as Purina Monster Chow."

"I'm sorry, Richie," panted Nat. "I came back to help you." Nat put the snake staff down to pull at the knot around Richie's feet. When he lifted Richie's legs, the rest of Richie's body fell off the coffee table and thumped to the floor.

"Owww!"

"Sorry!" Nat worked madly at the knot.

The Thin Man appeared in the doorway, grinning as he watched the two boys, then he motioned with a bony hand.

The fireplace poker levitated, found its bearings, and descended, whacking Nat over the head. Nat yelped in pain. He groped for the snake staff. The poker swung again. This time Nat waved his hand, and the poker veered off course.

Richie watched Nat deflect the poker with wide eyes as he worked to get loose from his bonds. Meanwhile, the Thin Man nonchalantly directed the poker with his dagger, like an amused conductor. He motioned to the coffee table, urging it to join the fray.

The coffee table rushed over and slammed into Nat's shins. Nat tumbled on top of the bucking table. It jerked left and right, looking for Nat, confused. Nat hopped to his feet, balancing atop the table as though riding a surfboard.

The poker wasn't as easily fooled as the table. The heavy metal rod was relentless, smashing holes in walls, floors, upholstery. Nat dodged, frantically waving the poker aside with the snake staff as he rode the table. When he saw his chance, Nat jumped off the stunned table, grabbed the edge, and flipped it over so that it flailed on its back like an overturned tortoise.

Richie had two hands free now.

Nat whirled. On his next parry, the snake staff coiled about the poker. Nat pulled it to the floor and stomped on it with his full weight. The poker bent severely in the middle. When Nat lifted his foot, it ran in harmless circles.

Demonkeeper

Nat twirled the staff. "Yeah!"

"Ahem," announced the Thin Man. He held Richie at knifepoint. "Playtime isss over." The Thin Man reached out with his hand. "Poisssonousss ssstick, if you pleassse, bottom end firssst."

When Nat hesitated, the Thin Man tickled Richie's chin with the knife, drawing a thin line of blood. "Okay, okay," Nat said. He slid the staff across the floor to the Thin Man.

The Thin Man moved the dagger away from Richie's throat. He grabbed the staff, pressed one thumb against the back of its head, snake-handler style, and produced a miniature apple from his pocket. He pushed it into the snake's mouth as a makeshift muzzle. Then he stuffed the full length of the snake into a pocket in his trench coat.

Nat stared, amazed. The man was good.

The Thin Man turned and pointed to a throw blanket on the couch. It might have been an ordinary blanket, except that the Thin Man's gesture sent it fluttering up into the air like a great bat. The blanket slithered toward Nat and wrapped him up where he stood just like the comforter that had snared Bel. Nat toppled to the ground.

Whump!

The Thin Man strode across the room to stand over Nat. He still held Richie tight.

Richie looked at Nat, wide-eyed. "Nat, what is this thing?"

"He's a mortal," Nat said, "same as you and me. But the chaos he's using is sucking the life out of him."

The Thin Man's eyes narrowed. "As I've sssaid, I'm working on that!" He dropped Richie back to the floor and felt for his knife. He rummaged in his pocket, perplexed. The knife was gone.

Richie leapt up, the ceremonial knife in his hand. He'd lifted it from the Thin Man's coat as slick as any street kid might pilfer a candy bar. He slashed the bonds around his ankles and brandished the weapon.

"Okay," he barked, "back off, you bony freak!"

The Thin Man stepped forward, undaunted, and glanced at the bookcase. Its books began to vibrate. He flipped his head. The bookcase spat a paperback at Richie—a four-by-seven-inch missile.

Richie waved the dagger, half out of instinct, half out of imitation of Nat. With a circular sweep of the weapon, he tried to will the book off course just as Nat had done with the poker. The book whipped by him, brushing his hair and denting the wall in a puff of hundred-year-old plaster. He'd pushed it slightly off course with his mind.

Richie grinned, impressed with himself. "Duuuude!" he said.

But he couldn't gloat for long. While he was distracted, the Thin Man pointed and nodded. The knife squirmed in Richie's hand. Richie tried to hold on, but it wrenched itself from his grasp and scooted across the floor to the Thin Man. "Fortusss," the Thin Man corrected him, "Ian Fortusss, not 'bony freak.'" He raised the knife.

Only just before Sandy struck from behind him did the Thin Man sense her presence. He turned in time to see her swing the heavy bag full of ash urns in a deliberate arc.

Whump!

The bag flattened the Thin Man, and the air filled with the ashes of many generations of Demonkeepers. Sandy groped toward Nat through the gray fog. Suddenly, the dagger glittered in the gloom, slashing and moving toward them. Sandy dragged Nat to the study window and boosted him up, still wrapped in his blanket cocoon. The Thin Man leapt for them, but just as he drew close, huge, vague fingers of ash rose up, grabbed the Thin Man, and slammed him to the ground.

Nat watched the swirling ash hand dissipate as quickly as it had appeared. He wondered if the dusty explosion of chaos had randomly chosen its victim or if it was somehow the souls of the Keepers helping him. It gave him heart to think that his forefathers might be taking his side.

Sandy was fumbling for the window and didn't see the ghostly hand in the gray cloud. "Out you go!" she announced, and she shoved Nat through.

CHAPTER 46

Everybody Run!

Nat flopped out onto the lawn outside still wrapped in the mad blanket. The blanket fell limp, and Nat rolled away, gasping for breath. With some effort, Nat turned his head to glare at the blanket.

"Hope you like it at Goodwill, Benedict Arnold," he said, coughing out a small gray cloud of his predecessors.

To Nat's astonishment, the ashes that had followed him out rose in the air, sorted themselves, and flew back inside through the window in small gray clouds. Sandy dropped from the window onto the grass beside Nat. "You came back," he wheezed.

Sandy stared after the ash, amazed to see it fly back into the house.

"Thank you," Nat continued. "I didn't think I had any friends who would risk so much for me."

"I want to help," she said, "but Richie's still in there with the creepy guy from downtown. Who is he?"

"Someone powerful," Nat panted, "someone evil. How'd you get inside?"

"The front door," she said.

"It let you in?"

She nodded.

Nat leapt to his feet and disappeared around the corner.

Sandy shook her head and ran after him.

• • •

Richie dashed down the hall toward the front door as the Thin Man appeared in the study doorway, dragging himself from the hazy grasp of the ash fingers that tore at him. As the fingers yanked at his coat, the snake staff slithered out of his pocket. It zipped off down the hall, fangs still stuck in the apple. In desperation, the Thin Man motioned ahead of Richie with his finger. "Ssstop him!"

The hall erupted with demons. A renegade chair trundled into Richie's path. Richie hurdled it. Nearby, the huge dining table clawed at the archway into the dining room with its thick talons, just barely unable to fit through and tear Richie limb from limb. Decorative trim boards scurried under his pumping feet. Richie ducked and dodged, leaping the smaller demons as he ran.

He tore across the room and threw open the front door, then stopped in his tracks.

A dark figure crouched on the porch, outlined in silhouette by the moonlight. At first, Richie thought it was Nat, but then he saw that it was too bulky. It also crouched on six limbs and sniffed about. Richie backed away. The shadow turned, and the yellow light of the moon fell on the grinning face of the Beast.

CHAPTER 47

Don't Go in the Basement . . . Again

The Beast sniffed the air and lowered its hungry gaze onto Richie, yellow claws flexing in and out. Richie stumbled backward as it stepped over the threshold. As if in league with the Beast, the front door swung closed behind it with the loneliest *clunk* Richie had ever heard.

Richie backed up against something and turned to find himself at the iron door to the basement. He shook his head.

"Nuh-uh, no way I'm going down there. . . ." He cowered, prepared to die where he stood.

But the Beast paused. It coughed, then spit up a hairball. The mucus-covered blob contained tangled green hair. Entwined in the green hair was Gus's skull-'n'-crossbones nose ring.

Richie whirled, threw open the basement door, and disappeared down the stairs.

The Beast approached and sniffed at the door to its former home. It paused, memories of decades in captivity battling raw hunger in its crude brain. Then it heard Richie yelp down below as he slipped on a step, and raw hunger won out. The Beast licked its lips and plunged into the darkness after him.

The Thin Man saw the Beast disappear into the darkness and smiled. "Oh, now thisss should be interessssting." He stepped through the basement door and descended at a leisurely pace.

CHAPTER 48

The Stairs

Sandy threw open the front door and held it for Nat as he scrambled across the heaving porch. The porch didn't attack her, but it bucked and writhed for Nat, ready to throw him off. Nat planted one foot on the top step, made a mighty leap, and dove through the door, rolling to his feet inside the house. He saw the open basement door immediately. He ran and looked down the stairs, then stepped back into the foyer and pushed the door shut with a *clang*, throwing the bolts home one after the other—*clack, clack, clack, clack, clack!*

"Ha! Ha ha!" He laughed. "I did it! I got you!"

Sandy walked up behind him. "Where's Richie?"

A boyish shout of alarm echoed up from the basement. Nat sighed and wrenched the bolts loose again.

Sandy grabbed him. "Nat, what's going on?"

Nat glanced around like a trapped animal. He shrugged. "Nothing?"

Just then, Pernicious scuttled past. Sandy's jaw dropped. The snake staff slithered from its hiding place and writhed over her foot on its way to Nat. She yelped and jumped. Then Nikolai thumped into the foyer holding the huge *DK Journal* over his head.

Nat stooped, grabbed the snake, and removed the apple from its mouth. The snake adjusted its sore jaw before stiffening into staff form. Nik held up the *Journal* for him. "Thanks, guys," Nat said.

He looked up at Sandy, who stared at him as though he too were as bizarre a monster as the creatures with which he kept company. He had to say something. "I, uh, keep demons in my house. It's a sort of wildlife preserve for monsters that cause chaos. The person you clobbered was an evil version of me who's trying to kill me so that he can use the demons to take over the world, and now he's in the basement with Richie and a huge man-eating Beast." He took a deep breath. "Don't tell anyone, okay?"

Sandy nodded mechanically, trying to process what Nat had just said.

Nat's eyes lit up. "Wait! You know Latin!"

Sandy nodded again, dumbstruck.

Nat pushed the *DK Journal* at her. "Here! Page fifteen hundred or so."

Sandy finally found her voice. "Here, what?"

"Look for something about 'the Beast,' then come down and tell me what it says." He turned and started down the stairs.

Sandy looked around, not about to go near the stairs. But Pernicious stood in the middle of the foyer, grinning up at her through his fangs. Nik approached and sniffed Sandy's foot with his pointed snout. That was enough for her. She ran after Nat.

Nat edged down the basement stairs. They were stone and carved right into the rock wall of the cavernous room. The walls were dimly lit by iridescent lichen, giving the whole place an eerie glow.

From what Nat could see, the open space below was bigger than the entire house above. The metal three-sided feeding chute hung in the dimness ten feet from the stairs. It spiraled down into the darkness below, like a slide out of a Dr. Seuss nightmare.

Sandy followed Nat, flipping through the *DK Journal.* After several steps, she squinted into the darkness and realized the vast expanse of the room.

"Oh my gosh! Nat, what is this?"

"I don't know."

"You don't know?"

"I've never been down here."

"It's getting too dark to read."

"Stay up here by the light. Keep reading. If you see anything strange, go back up and bolt the door." Then Nat plunged farther into the darkness.

Sandy stopped and closed the *Journal*. "If?"

Moments later Nat whispered up from below, "Still reading?"

Sandy hurried the *Journal* back open and lied quickly. "Yes."

Nat had taken several anxious steps on the crude stairs, and he still couldn't see the floor far below. Some of the stones underfoot were broken. He began to wonder how far he would fall if he took a wayward step.

"Here it is!"

Nat jumped and threw himself against the wall, his heart hammering in his chest.

The voice was Sandy's. "About the Beast," she said, "I found something!"

Nat exhaled heavily as she began to read to him from the dimness above. "'The chaos of the streets has become a Beast that we call the Killer of Lost Children. It might eat any of us that wander into its path, but stray children appear its natural prey. It rises from our roads to devour our refugees and runaways, our outcasts and orphans, and yet we cannot see it.'" Sandy glanced up. "Is that what you're looking for?"

Nat's mind spun. Orphans and runaways? *Of course,* he thought, *that's why it's after Richie!* He turned and whispered loudly to Sandy, "Is there anything else? An incantation?"

"No."

"A poem?"

"No."

"A short limerick?"

"No. Nothing like that."

Nat took another step. The hairs on the back of his neck twitched. He looked up. Crouched on a ledge ahead of him was the Beast.

CHAPTER 49

The Basement

Nat backed up the stairs, away from the ledge where the Beast crouched, lying in wait.

"Was that helpful?" Sandy called from above, oblivious.

"Not exactly," Nat muttered to himself.

"Nat?" called Sandy. "Nat? Do you need the book?"

Nat began to move more quickly up the stairs. Then he heard something and stopped.

"Nat . . . ?" It was Richie's voice. It came from far down the stairs.

The Beast still sat on the ledge, motionless, waiting for its victim to come within pouncing range.

Richie emerged from the shadows, edging up the stairs toward it. He didn't see the Beast.

"Nat . . . ?" he repeated. He saw Nat on the stairs above him and quickened his pace.

"Wait," Nat hissed.

Richie stopped, puzzled. Nat nodded covertly toward the Beast's hiding place.

Then Richie saw it waiting in ambush. He'd stopped only a step from being pounced upon. He looked up at Nat, defeated, scared, and sorry for the many things he'd done in his life for which he didn't have time to apologize.

Nat motioned for Richie to stay put while he spoke. "Richie," he said, taking a deep breath, "whatever happens, I want you to know two things. Thing one, you're not bait."

Richie nodded, bravely holding back a tear.

"And thing two. You have a home. You can stay here with me if you want to."

Richie looked around. He thought for a moment, then grinned through his fear. "This isn't gonna be my room, is it?"

Nat grinned back. In a gentle, even voice he said, "Walk up the stairs, and when I say 'go,' run for the door."

Richie eyed the Beast, which was up the stairs from him. "Up?"

"I just need a moment," Nat said. "Trust me."

"You sure you know what you're doing?"

Nat thought for a moment, then nodded. "When you get to the top, shut the door and lock it, and don't open it, no matter what you hear."

Richie nodded back and took a tentative step upward. His single, solitary step got the Beast's full attention. The massive creature dropped onto the stairs, facing Richie. Its bulk blocked out the light from the door above as it loomed over him. The Beast had only to lash out with its terrible claws and Richie's young breath would be snatched from him forever.

But it didn't pounce at once. It hesitated and sniffed Richie, its snout so close to him that Richie could feel its hot breath on his face.

The Beast puzzled over him for a moment, curious that he no longer smelled so lost, no longer smelled strongly of runaway nor smelled so deliciously orphaned. Richie stood petrified as the Beast decided that it would eat him anyway, but its pause was long enough. Nat leapt and hit the Beast with a flying tackle from behind, driving it over the side of the stairway.

Richie saw two tangled shadows disappear over the edge. He heard Nat's voice fade into the darkness below. "Go-ooooo!"

Richie flew past Sandy, grabbing her and dragging her along with him.

"Wait!" she cried.

"C'mon," Richie said, "I have orders."

Sandy stared back over her shoulder into the gloom as Richie hustled her out through the door.

Deep in the basement, Nat executed a one-point landing no better than his dismount from the viaduct earlier that night.

Wham!

He tried to rise but collapsed back to his hands and knees, his bones and muscles screaming their discontent with his insistence on jumping from high places. He groaned to himself. "Twice in one day?"

Flumph! The Beast landed lightly nearby, distributing the impact among all of its powerful limbs.

Clang! The door above swung shut. Nat rolled over, his back in agony. Gasping, Nat dragged himself backward. His head bumped against the feeding chute, and he looked up. The open, trough-shaped chute twisted upward and disappeared into the darkness above, rising toward the unseen trapdoor.

Quietly, the Thin Man approached from behind the Beast. He'd been watching from below, waiting for the Beast to come out into the open. He stared in awe as it loomed over Nat.

"Oh, my, look at it. It isss as amazing as I have

dreamed! It hidesss like a chameleon, tracksss like a bloodhound, and it killsss. Oh yesss, dead, dead, dead. I will make it . . . my asssasssin."

The Beast turned, suddenly noticing the Thin Man. The Thin Man stepped closer, still staring at it.

Seeing the Thin Man approach, Nat realized something. *He doesn't know,* he thought. Nat tried to wave the Thin Man away. "Wait! Dhaliwahl never told you what it eats!"

"Bah," the Thin Man scoffed. "It will eat what I sssay and like it . . . you, for instanccce."

"Listen to me!" Nat pleaded. "My duty is to help keep demons from harming people, even you."

At this, the Thin Man laughed long and loud. "You? Help me?"

The Beast crouched between them, drooling and considering them both, debating. But the Thin Man spoke louder.

"I need the help of no one!" he barked. "I have been on my own sssince I was twelve yearsss old, and today I ssstand alone at the very threshold of my childhood dream. Today I become the Demon Massster. And no bumbling boy apprentisss is going to trick me out of it!" He grinned. "I think I shall tessst my new sssoldier's feroccccity by having it pull out your entrailsss and ssstring them about like Chrissstmasss lightsss. Thisss place needsss a little sssomething, and I tend to be rather visssceral when it comesss to decorating."

The Beast turned fully toward the Thin Man. The Thin Man waved the dagger like a wand.

"Ah, I sssee that I have your attention, brute. Good." The Thin Man began his incantation. "Creature of Chaosss, hear my name . . ."

The Beast crept toward him as he recited, like an animal stalking prey.

Nat gasped. "No, Ian, look out!" Nat leapt forward to help, brandishing the snake staff, but the Beast threw a massive paw at Nat without even looking, backhanding him across the forehead. Nat flew and landed in a crumpled pile.

"I am Ian Fortusss," continued the Thin Man, "to you, your massster."

The Beast didn't stop. It raised its thick, hairy limbs. The Thin Man raised his own thin arms.

"Your massster!" he insisted.

The Beast kept coming. As the Beast neared, the Thin Man's confidence visibly faltered. He watched, perplexed, as the Beast grew larger and larger. And Nat watched as the Thin Man began to grow smaller and smaller.

Nat realized what the Thin Man was becoming. He was morphing into his childhood self, little Ian Fortus.

Demonkeeper

In a few horrifying moments, the gaunt menace that had challenged Nat with supreme confidence reverted to a terrified twelve-year-old boy in a baggy trench coat that puddled about his oversized shoes. Without his mentor, he'd never grown up. It hurt Nat to see Ian's childhood eyes, because they were clear now, and he could see regret in them. But now was too late.

Twelve-year-old Ian gazed up at the Beast. He clutched the big knife with two hands, holding it out before him like a crucifix against evil.

"No," whispered Nat to himself, "you're not its master. To the Beast, you're just . . ."

Sensing Ian's fear, the Beast pounced.

Nat covered his eyes. ". . . a runaway."

The Beast struck hard and fast. Ian had no time to react with more than a lost look of loneliness before the massive, hairy horror landed on him with an awful *crunch*.

Nat grimaced and struggled to his feet, leaning against the feeding chute. There were wet munching sounds. Nat couldn't watch. But as he turned away from the doomed runaway, he suddenly realized . . . *and I'm an orphan.*

CHAPTER 50

The Demonkeeper

As the Beast fed noisily between Nat and the stairs, Nat stumbled away from the chute. He began to move around the huge room, looking for another way out. He found only sheer walls until he spotted a trail of splintered white bones, which led to a small cave. With no other choice, he ducked inside.

The cave's stone walls were worn smooth by years of crude, persistent work. Nat moved farther in to look more closely. There was a mound of soft dirt with bones scattered about it. A nest. He shuddered as he realized the room was the Beast's lair. It smelled putrid, as though years of decay had been waiting to pounce upon the first visitor. Fish remains tangled in tufts of discarded fur lay scattered among piles of wet refuse that might have been recently regurgitated meals or extra-dimensional dung.

Nat almost turned and ducked out through the entrance. But there was something very out of place near the back of the small cave. Nat moved deeper into the lair, and beside the nest of bones he found a torn red garment.

He lifted the silk cloth and saw that it had Japanese characters. Nat suddenly recalled the legend of the man who had tried to handle the Beast and realized that he held the robe of that famed Keeper in his teenage hands. "Yatabe the Wanderer," Nat gasped. Now it was clear: Yatabe had sacrificed himself to lure the child-killing Beast down here into its prison. Young Raja Dhaliwahl would have been the grief-stricken apprentice who had to lock the door behind his own mentor and the Beast to complete the capture. For the first time, Nat fully understood his mentor's loneliness—the death of his teacher and the loss of his first pupil were why he had waited so long to recruit Nat. They were also the reasons he advised against having friends or caring for a girl. He was simply afraid of losing anyone he was close to.

Nat heard snuffling sounds outside the cave. The Beast had finished with Ian. Nat clutched the red garment and glanced about. Nowhere to run.

Outside the cave, the Beast closed in on the entrance, grinning, still hungry, ever hungry. It could smell a lingering scent of orphan inside with a hint of doubt. But as it closed in on the trapped prey that had wandered into its very lair, it stopped and sniffed. The Beast sniffed again, perplexed. Just as had happened with the boy on the stone stairs, the scent had suddenly weakened. The Beast had always trusted its bloodhound snout, but something was wrong now.

Nat emerged wearing Yatabe's red robe and brandishing the snake staff like a whip. He stood tall and set his feet wide in case the Beast charged.

The Beast hesitated, for it no longer smelled scared orphan boy. What had gone into the cave was not the same as what came out. The person who faced it now was a formidable young man in full Demonkeeper dress.

Nat looked directly into the Beast's narrow, bloodshot eyes and spoke in a deep, commanding voice. "Hear my words," he intoned, "for I am your Keeper." Nat raised the staff. "And this is my house!"

For a moment, the Beast cowered, hearing the conviction in Nat's voice and wary of the writhing snake in his hand, which it sensed was a powerful creature of its own type.

But as soon as Nat saw that he had backed the Beast off, his thoughts turned to escape. He glanced away for a moment, looking for a chance to maneuver around it.

In that moment, the Beast smelled doubt and rose

up again. It roared and sent Nat diving for cover with a sweep of one massive arm.

The Beast's speed shocked Nat, and he avoided decapitation only by throwing himself backward. The Beast no longer hesitated as it had on the stairs. It stomped through the splinters of bones toward him. In desperation, Nat thrust out the snake staff.

Coming fast and too eager to avoid it, the Beast ran right into the wedge-shaped head of the staff. The snake sank its fangs into one hairy limb, and the Beast howled in agony. It seized the snake with a free claw and yanked Nat up, swinging him through the air.

Nat flew into the feeding chute. *Clang!* He hit the dirt and rolled over, dazed, expecting to find the Beast looming over him, ripping and tearing at him with tooth and claw. But the massive creature still stood where it had been bitten. It stared down at its limp, injured limb, grunting in pain.

Nat stared too. He had watched Dhaliwahl carry the snake staff for years. Ian Fortus had feared it. Though Nat knew that the mysterious staff was powerful, he'd never seen it used. He didn't know what it could do. He watched in wonder as the Beast's arm began to disintegrate into dust.

"Whoa!"

In moments the furry arm was gone. Nat thought for a crazy moment that if he could just hit the Beast five more times, it would have no limbs with which to chase him. But the Beast growled and leapt after Nat with its remaining limbs and frothing jaws.

Nat struggled to his feet, raising the snake staff, but it was too late. The Beast's first blow took Nat in the side. He felt a sharp pain. The second glanced off his head, shearing a patch of hair from his scalp. Nat landed in a heap again, holding his ribs.

The Beast leapt to finish him off. Nat raised the staff as high as he could. But instead of striking, the staff looped itself around the feeding chute overhead. At the last possible moment, it pulled Nat up into the air.

The Beast charged by beneath him, waving the stump of its absent arm up at Nat as he yanked his feet up out of its path. With the aid of the living rope, he began to struggle up the feeding chute like a desperate rock climber.

•   •   •

Sandy turned toward the trapdoor. "Richie, I hear something here. Maybe it's Nat!" Sandy knelt and reached for the single, heavy bar.

Richie put his ear to the basement door, listening carefully. "No, it's coming from over here." Richie began to open the door.

Demonkeeper

The Beast crouched on the other side of the door. It had tracked Nat, climbing up the crumbling stairs as Nat climbed the chute nearby. But now it heard the bolt begin to slide open. It grinned and turned its attention to the door.

Sandy released the bar on the trapdoor and eased it open. Suddenly, a snake darted from the chute. It coiled around her wrist and yanked her forward. She gasped and braced herself, sitting over the chute so that only her splayed legs kept her from plummeting into the basement. Sandy looked down between her knees to see Nat clinging to the chute, bruised like an overripe banana, bleeding, and filthy dirty. The other end of the snake was wrapped around his wrist.

"Pull!" he pleaded. She began to lift with all her might.

Richie glanced over and saw Sandy pulling. He smiled, seeing Nat's arms reach up through the trapdoor, but that meant something else was at the basement door with him, and he had opened all but one bolt. . . .

Whang!

The door shuddered, and Richie's ear rang as though someone had clapped a cymbal on the side of his head.

Whang-whang! The door shuddered again.

Richie fell back, the sound echoing in his skull.

Wham-wham-wham!

Richie stared. The last inch of the loose bolt was still seated in the lock. It began to bend under the furious, furry assault from the other side of the door.

The Beast howled and pounded on the door. Richie crawled away, unable to bring himself to reach for the bolt, which rattled precariously in its lock as the Beast assaulted the door. Finally, it shook loose.

"Look out," Richie cried to Sandy, "it's coming through!"

Nat saw the danger. He let go of Sandy's helping hand and slid back down into the basement, clinging to the feeding chute.

The Beast was pounding on the door ten feet away in the darkness. "Hey," Nat yelled at it, "over here! I'm the orphan. I'm the one you want. Nobody cares for me!"

The Beast roared. It turned and leapt across the ten-foot space between the stairs and the hanging metal trough. The massive creature hit the chute just below Nat and clamped on with its five good limbs. The chute shuddered and swayed as the Beast scrabbled for purchase, straining upward with one free claw for Nat's dangling foot.

Nat looked down. He'd used all his strength to climb the chute. He didn't have the energy to pull himself back up now. The Beast's talon was inches from his foot. He closed his eyes, preparing to be pulled down into the darkness, devoured finally by the killer of the orphaned and lost, just as Yatabe the Wanderer had been so many years ago.

Then he heard a groan of tortured metal giving way. The chute shifted beneath him, failing under the combined weight of Nat and the Beast. It separated from the floor above and tumbled into the darkness, right out from under the Beast. The Beast stared upward as it began to fall. Its snarl faded into a blank look of surprise as the gloom swallowed it up. It faded into the depths of the basement until even its malevolent yellow saucer eyes were gone.

Nat swung freely over the abyss, held now only by Sandy and the snake. Worn and beaten, his own muscles proved useless now. He heard the distant clattering din of the chute collapsing into a pile of scrap metal somewhere far below and a very painful-sounding *clang* as the Beast landed in the middle of it.

EPILOGUE

Sandy and Richie pulled, struggling to haul Nat up.
Nik leapt in to help, grabbing Sandy's belt loop. He
yanked hard, and Nat's limp body spilled up through
the opening. They tumbled backward into a sweaty pile
of humans and demons.

As Nat, Sandy, Richie, the snake staff, and Nik
fought to untangle themselves, Bel wandered over and
pushed the trapdoor shut. The heavy dog stood on it
until Richie crawled over and threw the bar.

Nat lay on his back, eyes closed, wheezing from his
titanic effort. The snake staff lay beside him, also gasping for breath. After a few moments, Nat opened his
eyes to find Sandy looking down at him. Her muscles
were taut, her glasses were off, and her hair was in disar-
ray. She looked wild and adventurous, not at all like the

normal, careful junior assistant librarian Nat had met two days earlier. Nat breathed heavily and motioned her closer. She leaned in.

"Yes?" she said expectantly.

"Bolt," Nat whispered, "the door."

Richie overheard and leapt up to secure the bolts on the basement door.

Sandy turned to Nat again. "I care, you weirdo." She smiled softly, and she leaned toward him.

Just then, Pernicious sprang between them, jumping up and down and clapping like a stuffed monkey with cymbals.

"Yee-hee-hee-heeee!"

• • •

Later that morning, Sandy and Nat sat on the porch. Richie leaned on the rail. In the window above, three little gargoyle faces crowded for a view.

"I don't know what to say, Nat," Sandy said. "I was terrified. Is this all real?"

Nat waved his hand, and the porch undulated, moving Sandy snugly against him. "You shouldn't even be here. You're not supposed to see any of this."

"What do you mean?"

Richie poked his head in. "Because you're a chick."

"Oh, really?" Sandy eyed Nat.

"No. It's because you're not a Keeper," Nat said.

"I kept you from getting killed."

"A Demonkeeper," Nat said.

"So you expect me just to walk away as if none of this whole adventure ever happened?"

"And it's incredibly important that you not tell anyone either."

Sandy smirked. "Who would believe me?" She stood and considered the glow of the oncoming dawn. "I'm going to be in the biggest trouble I've ever been in," Sandy said. "This is not the way people expect a girl like me to behave."

Nat slumped. "I understand."

Sandy straightened her clothes and hair, donned her glasses, and smiled. "Then again, this has been the most exciting weekend I've ever had in my life."

Nat cocked his head and brightened. "You know, it's going to take a little time to get things back to abnormal around here, but when I do, um . . . ."

Sandy leapt forward and hugged him. "I'm going to be so grounded, but I can sneak away from school at lunchtime!"

There was an awkward silence as they hugged. Sandy pulled her head back and looked into Nat's dark eyes, waiting. Richie waited. The demons in the window waited. Everybody waited. Finally, left with no other apparent alternative, Nat leaned in and kissed her.

Above, Flappy and Nik put their hands over their eyes. Pernicious stared, tongue lolling like a New Year's noisemaker until Flappy put a wing over his eyes too.

Nat and Sandy held the kiss until the sun peeked over the horizon at them. Finally, with great reluctance, Nat pulled his lips from hers. "Go ahead." He nodded. "Like I said, I have some things to sort out here. But I'll see you soon . . . real soon."

Sandy gave him the "are-you-sure?" look. Nat nodded. Sandy ruffled Richie's hair as she walked down the steps and away. Halfway across the lawn, she turned to take another disbelieving look at the house. The demons grinned at her from the windows. She waved, shook her head, and skipped off toward her car.

Nat watched her go. Dhaliwahl had been right: the distraction Sandy had caused had been a disaster. But his mentor had been wrong too. Girls weren't the problem. The chaos had arisen from Nat's own fearful attempts to keep Sandy *out* of his world. When he finally let her in, she'd actually rescued him. And she was awfully cute without her thick glasses.

Richie watched Nat watch Sandy. "Dude, what are you doing? She's getting away."

"This is where I belong," Nat said. "I have duties,

responsibilities." His head swayed in sync with Sandy's receding walk. "You familiar with those?"

"But you really dig her, don't you?"

"Yes," Nat said, "she's normal."

"Normal? Man, she's awesome!"

"Yeah, that too."

"Then you gotta close the deal!"

Nat turned. "Patience and confidence, Richie, like keeping demons."

Richie nodded. "You know, I was wondering . . . can you teach me that?"

"Confidence?"

"I was actually talking about keeping demons and the other cool stuff," Richie said.

"Are you sure a kid like you wants responsibility?"

Richie didn't answer at first. When he did, he chose his words carefully. "Uh, well, what I kinda want is just . . ." He thought for a moment. ". . . to be more like you."

Nat stood and considered Richie, his new apprentice. His voice felt deeper than it had only a day earlier. "All right, then, young Richard." Nat stepped across the threshold and turned. "Follow me." He motioned Richie inside.

Richie stood staring into the shadowy house.

Behind Nat, a thousand yellow eyes stared back.

Nikolai and Pernicious stood on either side of the entry like solemn guards. Flappy swooped in and perched stoically over the door. Trundling up last, Bel took his place next to Nat, who rested a hand on his head.

Richie took a deep breath and entered, walking with them into the darkness.